No Dogs Allowed

Farrar Straus Giroux
New York

JANE CUTLER

No Dogs Allowed

Pictures by
TRACEY CAMPBELL PEARSON

Contents

No Dogs Allowed

No Dogs

Jason and Edward Fraser wanted a dog. But their parents said they couldn't have one.

"Because you're both allergic," their mother explained. "Allergies and dogs just don't mix."

The boys walked glumly into the family room.

"I guess that's life," said Jason, who was eight.

"Rrrowf, rrrowf, grrr, ruf-ruf-ruf!" said Edward, who was almost six.

"Very funny," said Jason.

"Name Tuffles," Edward said, in a voice that sounded a little like his own voice and a little like the sort of voice a young, friendly dog might have.

"What?" asked Jason.

"Tuffles, rrrowf, *Tuffles*," replied Edward, scrambling around the family room floor on his hands and knees.

"Edward, stand up," said Jason.

Edward sat back on his heels and held his hands in front of his chest, like paws. He grinned and rolled his eyes. Then he panted: "Pant, pant!"

Jason walked away.

Edward followed, grabbing at Jason's heels.

"Quit that, Edward," Jason said.

"Rrrowf, *Tuffles*," Edward insisted.

Jason went into the back yard, and Edward followed on his hands and knees. A yellow tennis ball was on the grass. Edward tucked it under his chin and dropped it at Jason's feet.

"Edward, I want you to stop this," Jason said, picking up the ball and tossing it away.

"Ruf!" Edward retrieved the ball. "Rrowf!" he demanded, "more!"

Jason stared hard at Edward. This time he picked up the ball and put it in his pocket.

Edward kept his friendly dog eyes on Jason's face. He ducked and dodged and woofed. "Chase Tuffles," he said. "Ruf! Ruf! Chase!"

Jason tried to ignore his brother. He sat down on the back steps and studied a tiny caterpillar slowly making its way along the edge of a stair.

When he got tired of watching the caterpillar, he leaned back and watched Edward digging wildly in the flower bed, spraying the loose dirt out behind him.

For a moment, Jason thought his brother looked more like a dog digging with his paws than like a boy digging with his hands. He closed his eyes and shook his head. Then he moved into the shade of the walnut tree.

As soon as Jason settled down comfortably on the grass, Tuffles charged over, put his dirty paws on Jason's chest, and licked his face.

"That does it!" Jason sprang to his feet and started after his brother.

Tuffles made for the back door. "Mom!" he called, in his regular voice. "Mom!"

Jason grabbed Edward's T-shirt and pulled him down onto the grass. They wrestled, rolling over and over.

When they got tired, they lay on their backs, side by side, breathing hard and looking up at the blue sky, trying to find shapes and faces in the clouds.

"I see a dragon," Edward said, pointing at a dragon-shaped cloud passing overhead.

Pretty soon their noses began to run. The boys were allergic to grass, too.

———

Late Monday afternoon, when Jason came home from his friend Jeffrey's house, Edward was hard at work drawing a picture on a large piece of paper. His Magic Markers were scattered around him on the floor.

Jason stopped to look at Edward's picture. It was divided in half. The top half showed a round-faced boy with teacup ears and a scribbly patch of brown hair. The boy looked out, frowning. "Edward" was printed next to him in rambling red letters.

The bottom half of the picture showed a sleepy-looking spotted dog with a small head and big paws. The dog stood sideways. His ears hung down and his tail stuck up. "Tuffles" was printed underneath.

"Pretty good," said Jason.

"Thanks," said Edward. "Mom helped me spell."

"She helped you spell Edward?" Jason teased.

"Spell Tuffles," Edward answered.

Both boys looked at the frowning Edward and at the sideways-standing Tuffles. "You're a good artist," Jason said.

Edward nodded. He threw his arms around Jason's leg. "Ruf! Ruf!" he cried. "Me Tuffles! Ruf!"

Jason walked all the way to his bedroom with

Tuffles hanging on to one leg. Then he shook him off. "Stay," he said firmly and closed his door.

From then on, Edward was Edward about half of the time, and the other half, he was Tuffles. Jason was surprised at how good-natured his parents were about this.

"You remind me of a dog I had when I was a boy," their dad said, holding Edward on his lap and scratching him behind the ears.

"Dog food!" their mother called, setting a sandwich down at Edward's place. "Enriched with all the vitamins and minerals a growing dog needs."

"Both of you are encouraging him," Jason grumbled.

"It's only a game, honey," his mom said. "There's no harm in it."

"If Edward really thinks he's a dog, there might be harm in it," Jason pointed out. "Besides, it bugs me."

"Edward doesn't really think he's a dog, Jason," replied his mom. "Edward knows he's not a dog, doesn't he, Tuffles?" she asked, patting Edward on the head.

"Ruf!" Edward answered.

———

The next day, Edward brought his friends Emma and Betsy home after kindergarten. Jason was home already. He had a cold, so he hadn't gone to school. He was building a model airplane at the table in the kitchen.

As soon as Edward and his friends came in, they began to bark and howl and yowl. They crawled around on the kitchen floor and climbed over each other and rolled on their backs. Then Edward crawled over to Jason and put one paw in Jason's lap. "Ruf?" he said.

Jason pushed Edward's hand off his lap. "Why don't you guys play outside," he suggested. "You don't want to catch my cold."

Barking and yapping, the three kindergartners scrambled out to the yard.

"What's all that noise?" Jason's mother asked, poking her head into the kitchen.

"Edward's home," Jason answered.

"Yes?" said Mrs. Fraser.

"He brought some friends," Jason said, carefully putting together two parts of the airplane's tail. "And they're playing Humane Society."

"Humane Society?" asked his mother.

"Lonely dogs," Jason explained, "waiting to be adopted. Edward made it up, and now he and his friends play it at school."

9

THE BOOKSELLER

FOR TEN YEARS, JEAN LOSSERAND HAD TRIED desperately to hold on to his thirst for life and adventure, but as time wore on, he became bitterly aware that he was losing interest in his quest for happiness. He had long dreamed of escaping this city that was like a prison, but as his hopes faded, so, too, did the strength to struggle against his fate. Now and then, he thought sadly of his aging mother and reflected that he would never see her again. His monotonous existence had stifled even his love of freedom, and his beloved books had finally lost their charm. Fairy tales, fantastic stories, and all novels had been forbidden. Only biographies or technical works were allowed, because they did not offend the Council. Jean Losserand could no longer find comfort anywhere; he was under constant surveillance and now lacked the willpower to fight back in any way. His life had been reduced to an endless, helpless sigh. Until the day he heard a knock on his shop door.

Since he had so few customers, he no longer bothered to take care of his bookshop, which looked neglected. Dusty, torn volumes were stacked everywhere in untidy piles, and the shop door was always closed, so he was surprised when someone came knocking. He shuffled slowly to the door, opened it, and stood gaping in astonishment at the three girls, who gazed back curiously at him.

"Are you Jean Losserand?" inquired Jade.

The bookseller studied her for a moment, noticing the liveliness and determination that danced in her eyes: the color of jade, he thought.

"Excuse us for disturbing you," said Amber softly, "but are you really Jean Losserand, the son of the old woman who lives in a remote farmhouse?"

"With a disgusting stable," added Jade.

"I am indeed Jean Losserand," said the startled man. "Do you know my mother?"

"Yes!" said Jade gaily. "She's very hospitable."

"My mother?" he repeated in disbelief.

"Yes," replied Jade. "We've come here to ask you for help. May we come in?"

"Of course."

Jean Losserand led the unexpected visitors to an adjoining room, where he invited them to sit down in some very worn, red velvet armchairs. He fussed around them, offering them biscuits, preparing mint tea, all the while studying them intently. Their clothes seemed quite ordinary, of good quality but not luxurious. In all other respects, however, the three girls were most unlike one another. When he looked into Amber's face, he seemed troubled, and his left hand began to shake the way it always did when he was overcome with emotion. Amber noticed that he had trouble setting the teapot down on a low table, and she served the mint tea for him, pouring it into chipped china cups.

"Thank you," he murmured gratefully. "And now, tell me what I can do for you."

"It's a long story," replied Jade.

Then she quietly and carefully inspected their surroundings. Taking a sip of piping hot tea, she spilled some on her trousers. Her sumptuous attire had been attracting unwelcome stares of amazement from the citizens of Nathyrnn, and Amber had finally convinced her, to sell her dress and some of her precious jewelry. Jade had used some of the money to buy more suitable clothing, and Amber had used a few small copper coins from her black velvet purse to purchase a plain, simple outfit, because even her peasant clothes had been attracting attention. She had also washed her face at a public fountain to get rid of the smudges of dirt, straw, and tears. Nibbling on a biscuit, Amber felt better, refreshed, even though she was exhausted; their communication with the Stones had sapped all her energy. She was relieved to have arrived at last at Jean Losserand's shop, which had been hard to find in the dark and narrow street. Amber had regretfully concluded that she did not like Nathyrnn: the people appeared surly and uncommunicative and the streets were too quiet, without many shops. Everything was shabby and deserted. She felt reassured to be in the bookshop, with this man who seemed friendly and attentive. She had observed him closely, as was her habit. He was impressively tall, but his shoulders drooped a little, as if he carried a heavy burden. Amber guessed that he was between thirty and forty years old. His face was stamped with wisdom and kindness, yet his eyes expressed a kind of resigned despair and regret.

"Explain how I can help you," he repeated. "Who are you? What are you doing in Nathyrnn?"

He seemed to be speaking to Amber, but it was Jade who replied.

"We come from the area around the palace of Divulyon, and we are here to see you. We were able to enter Nathyrnn thanks to Opal's brilliant lie."

Jade jerked her chin at Opal with a hint of disdain, and Opal returned the favor with an icy look.

"We know you are on our side," continued Jade, " and we have enemies in common." In a low voice, she added, "It seems the Council of Twelve is meeting to talk about us. And what they have to say is not good. . . ."

"If you are enemies of the Council of Twelve, then welcome to Nathyrnn. This city is really a prison where those who have visited Fairytale are held captive," explained Jean Losserand.

"We don't have any idea why the council is concerned with us," confided Amber, "and we have enemies whose identities we don't even know. Just today Opal received a terrifyingly powerful and evil telepathic message. Do you know who could have done this?"

"Only the members of the Council of Twelve know how to practice telepathy. In Fairytale, of course, many magicians can perform it as well, but they could never have sent a message from such a great distance."

"Then the Council of Twelve really is against us," observed Jade. "I can't believe it. I've never heard anything bad about the Council of Twelve. My own father was chosen to govern a territory and was made a duke by the council. He obeys the laws and the orders of those twelve old men."

Seeing Jean Losserand's puzzled expression, Jade explained herself.

"I am Jade of Divulyon. I shouldn't really tell you this, but I trust you. I found out just recently that I'm not the duke's daughter after all, and I've been driven from the palace."

The bookseller was beginning to understand. So, the rumors that had already been circulating in Fairytale ten years before had been well founded. All his doubts about Amber suddenly became certainties. He had recognized her—she was indeed who he thought she was. He had studied every feature of her face, and his suspicions were confirmed. Jean Losserand was filled with joy: *she* was alive! The sun rose in his heart, as hope and an infinite love of life flooded back into his soul. He told himself once more, *She is alive!* He was burning to shout out those wondrous words, but he knew that he must not, and managed to hold his tongue.

Meanwhile, Jade was looking in her bag for the paper on which she had drawn the symbol. When she finally found it, she gave it to Jean Losserand, who examined it with interest.

"What is it?" asked Jade breathlessly. "Can you understand it?"

"It's a sign written in one of the ancient languages of Fairytale," he said immediately.

"Really!" exclaimed Amber. "And what does it mean?"

"It's rather complicated—it concerns wisdom and the power to read what is hidden deep within the heart, but at the same time, the symbol can be read as a name: Oonagh."

"Oonagh?" repeated Amber, instantly enchanted by the lilting sound of the name.

"Oonagh is someone who lives in Fairytale," continued the bookseller, "someone whose people have been largely decimated by the Council of Twelve. Oonagh is a magic creature renowned for her wisdom, and she can read the secrets of the heart. She is spoken of with the greatest respect."

"Oonagh lives in Fairytale!" breathed Amber, her imagination catching fire.

"Yes, in a crystalline grotto."

"I think we'll have to go and visit this Oonagh," observed Jade. "But tell us a little about Fairytale. I thought it was a legend."

"Not at all," Jean Losserand assured them. "I really did go there."

"Well—what's this place like?" asked Jade.

"I'll tell you everything I know. But, most important,

to be able to cross the magnetic field surrounding Fairytale, you must believe wholeheartedly in the impossible. You girls are no longer naive children trusting in fantasy, so this may be difficult for you."

"I'll manage it," said Jade haughtily, because she couldn't conceive of anything in the world that she would not be able to do.

"Who lives in Fairytale?" asked Amber. "Damsels in distress, knights in shining armor, wizards?"

"Among others. A long, long time ago, when the Council of Twelve did not yet have the power it wields now, hundreds of people with magic powers lived freely in the world. Human beings were merely one of many advanced species, and everyone respected their mutual differences. Yet despite the many advances humankind had made—technological progress, huge towering cities, travel to the stars—the Council of Twelve feared the immense power these kindly magic creatures held. The council gained power by sowing hatred in men's hearts against the other races. Gradually, by abusing the trust of those peoples who were so different from us, the council succeeded in destroying them. It was a lawless time, and a shameful one, too."

A shadow of fear passed over Amber's gentle face.

"What happened next?" she asked haltingly. "Why didn't anyone rise up and try to save them?"

"No one really understood what was going on. People trusted their neighbors and were used to living in harmony. It all happened in a confused and secretive way. Finally, the magic creatures, who were peaceful beings, decided to avoid further bloodshed. Their survivors withdrew into a distant land, far from civilization, but rich and fertile. There they combined their powers and created magnetic fields to protect themselves. Thus was born Fairytale, which has now become a prosperous country of entrancing beauty, where humans and creatures endowed with supernatural powers live side by side with the same tolerance as before. Unfortunately, evil does rage there as well. Wherever there is life, there cannot be only goodness. But at least the Council of Twelve is unable to impose its law there. It is a free place."

"That story is so beautiful," murmured Amber, deeply moved.

"Yes," said Jade matter-of-factly. "Is Fairytale far from here?"

"No, it's not far at all," replied Jean Losserand. "Nathyrnn marks the limit of the dukedom of Divulyon. The border is less than fifteen minutes away, but heavily guarded. Few succeed in crossing it. And just beyond lie the magnetic fields surrounding Fairytale."

"That close?" cried Jade. "Then it will be easy to get there."

"No, it won't. To begin with, you need an exit pass to leave Nathyrnn. Then comes the hardest part: crossing the border."

"Getting out of Nathyrnn shouldn't be a problem: Opal thought up a very plausible lie," remarked Jade acidly. She was still disgruntled at failing to win over the Knight of the Order through her own scheme.

"Yes," agreed Amber enthusiastically—"Tell him, Opal!"

Reluctantly, Opal did.

"Some instinct led me to say that I was working for the Council of Twelve," she related in an indifferent voice. "I was suddenly convinced that the telepathic message had come from them. I knew, I sensed, that we were their enemies."

At these words, Jean Losserand shivered.

"It is true that when a message is sent telepathically, the mind of the person sending the message must be linked to the mind of the person receiving it. However, that does not mean that they can read each other's thoughts," he said. "Unless—unless the purpose of the message is to instill fear or inflict pain."

There was an uneasy silence.

"The voice also spoke of a prophecy," said Amber faintly. "And an enormous book covered with blood. Do you know what that's all about?"

Jean Losserand weighed his words carefully, afraid of revealing what it was vital to conceal. Before he replied, he considered Amber for a moment, with her sweet face and kind eyes.

"*The Prophecy* was written centuries ago by a philosopher named Néophileus, who was a member of a strong and unconquerable fairy race called the Clohryuns. Néophileus had the gift of seeing into the future, and he had a premonition that many of his kind would be destroyed, a few hundred years later, by the Council of Twelve. Unfortunately, no one believed him, because everyone thought that they had learned to live in peace forever."

The three girls were transfixed by his words: Jade's eyes gleamed with curiosity, and Amber's reflected interest and understanding, while Opal's remained inscrutable.

"Néophileus also felt that a day would come when times would change and the world would be transformed. He foretold a deep disturbance, but for the first time in his life, his powers failed him, and he was unable to decipher any details."

"I don't understand," said Amber.

"In other words, at a certain place on the curve of time, the future was unclear to Néophileus. He saw that instead of following a single, distinct line, the future divided at that particular point into several paths. Only one path would be taken, and all of humanity would follow a course that would change the world as we know it. And so, Néophileus wrote *The Prophecy*."

Jean Losserand stopped. He had said enough.

"We absolutely must go to Fairytale to consult Oonagh," said Amber. "How can we cross the border of Divulyon?"

"I don't know what to advise you," confessed the bookseller. "When I went to Fairytale, the border existed only in theory. Now, it's quite a different matter."

"We'll get across," said Jade confidently.

"How?" insisted Amber.

"I cannot help you," replied Jean Losserand, "but go and see a young man called Adrien of Rivebel. He is only sixteen, but he has already spent three years in Nathyrnn's dungeons. And he has just been set free."

"But why was he locked up?" cried Amber.

"This young man lived in Fairytale, where he was born the son of a noble family of knights. When he was thirteen, Adrien wanted to explore the outside world, so he left his homeland. The Knights of the Order seized him at the border of Divulyon and threw him in prison."

"That's not fair!" exclaimed Amber.

"Of course not," agreed Jean Losserand. "But rumor has it that he isn't like the other prisoners. Locking him away hasn't broken his spirit at all. In fact, people say that he's indomitable and that the bars of his cell, far from destroying him, have toughened him instead. He has been condemned to spend his life here, in this grim and hopeless city, yet everyone is saying that he's trying to incite a rebellion to liberate the citizens of Nathyrnn."

"I love rebellions!" crowed Jade. "What a good idea."

"Unfortunately, it's impossible," sighed the bookseller.

"No," said Amber. "Nothing is impossible."

Jean Losserand smiled sadly. He no longer had the heart to dream of the impossible.

"Go and see Adrien of Rivebel," he repeated. "Perhaps he can help you."

Jade tossed back a stray lock of black hair and said, "We don't need any help, but we'll go and see this Adrien of Rivebel. Nathyrnn must be liberated."

"I'm telling you, it's impossible," groaned the book-seller.

"Your mother is waiting for you, Mr. Losserand," replied Jade, "and I promised to send her news of you. The best thing would be if you took it to her yourself, don't you think?" And she added defiantly, "Nothing is impossible!"

10

ADRIEN OF RIVEBEL

AMBER EXPECTED TO SEE A CHARMING PRINCE straight out of a fairy tale, gallant and poetic, but Adrien looked more like a young knight with hard, chiseled features. He seemed thoughtful and self-possessed, and only his grave eyes revealed the courage and fire that burned inside him. His tousled chestnut hair added to the aura of brooding mystery that surrounded him. Adrien knew how to feign indifference and disguise his deepest feelings: that was what had enabled him to withstand those three years of prison. He had not committed any crime, but rather than allowing himself to be overcome by fury, he had survived by holding on to the knowledge that his conscience was clear. Realizing that anger was useless, he had ignored it, even though in his heart he cried out for justice. Now that he was free again, he had let his true nature reassert itself. He had planned the revolt of Nathyrnn down to the last detail, and now he was seeking allies to join his cause. He was sure that his plan would succeed, but he had yet to find anyone who could help him carry it out. Almost all the inhabitants of Nathyrnn had been "broken," either by prison, or simply by habit and submissiveness. There were not many left who held on to their hopes and dreams. Only a few approved of Adrien's revolt, but even they did not dare to join him. They were not won over—yet.

So Adrien of Rivebel had not despaired, but he was still waiting for help. It came to him in an unlikely form when he met Jade, Opal, and Amber. He was not in the least surprised to see them burst into his tiny room at the inn where he was staying, and he welcomed them cordially, waving them toward some rickety chairs. Adrien of Rivebel was educated and intelligent: he had known at once who his visitors were, for he had heard many stories about them in Fairytale. He himself, on his tenth birthday, had consulted Oonagh to learn what path he should follow, and the magic creature had advised him: "You are not the Chosen One. But you cannot remain in the shadows. Your heart is proud and passionate: find water to dampen that devastating ardor, not fuel to kindle its flames."

"But why?" Adrien had asked in disappointment.

"You are capable of provoking great danger. You must be extremely careful, or other lives will be placed in peril. Do not listen to your heart—it is too impetuous.

Open your eyes and be guided by your reason."

"This is all very confusing," Adrien had murmured.

"One day you will encounter those whom all are waiting for, and you will understand."

Now that the three Stones of the Prophecy were standing before him, he was not sure what lay ahead, but he had a clear sense that together they would be able to take a step in the right direction. Of course, he said nothing of all of this to them.

At first the girls studied him in silence. They each soon recognized him as someone they could trust: the one person who could help them escape Nathyrnn and enter Fairytale.

Jade understood immediately that she had found an ally, someone like herself. In his eyes she read the revolt of Nathyrnn that she might organize with him. She paid no attention to the intensity with which Adrien returned her gaze, but it did not escape either Amber or Opal.

Amber was impressed by the young man. She guessed that he was headstrong and determined, like Jade, but capable of much more self-control. Opal's reaction had been different: the very instant she laid eyes on Adrien, a profound change came over her. She was deeply affected, and experienced a sudden warmth spreading through her being; she could not resist this feeling and, if the truth be told, she did not wish to. She felt pleasantly strange, and wondered vaguely what was happening to her. She stared openly at Adrien's face. And then it came to her: she understood, she knew, that she was made to love those gray-green eyes. She was certain that she and Adrien should be together—it could not be otherwise. She, who was normally so cold, was flushed with warmth. But Adrien's eyes were riveted on Jade. Opal saw this, yet felt no jealousy, no resentment. It's a mistake, she thought calmly. Adrien cannot look at Jade that way. And if he's feeling for her what I feel for him, then . . . he'll have to change his mind.

Meanwhile, delighted at the prospect of stirring up a revolt, of defying the law and proving her bravery, Jade had launched into an excited discussion about the uprising in the city.

"A friend has told us that you're plotting revolution in Nathyrnn!" she told Adrien, flashing him a knowing smile.

She addressed him with easy familiarity. He was only two years older than she was, and politeness had never been her strong point.

"I don't want to spend my life within the walls of this horribly sad city," replied Adrien. "I've come up with a plan of escape, to return to Fairytale. But I want *all* the inhabitants of Nathyrnn to be free. And I know I can do it, although it's quite complicated. We would have to use magic, but I haven't found anyone in this city capable of accomplishing what I have in mind."

"And what's that?" said Jade impatiently.

"Someone must cast a spell, and all those who find themselves outside the magic circle must be put into a deep sleep."

"What is a magic circle?"

"It's a small protective spell circle that forms around a sorcerer when he recites magic formulae, to shield him from the effects of his own magic. When he casts a sleep spell, the circle helps him to stay awake. Once the circle is formed and the recital is finished, the sorcerer may leave the circle without being affected by the spell."

"I see the problem," mused Jade. "The Knights of the Order would fall asleep, but so would the inhabitants of Nathyrnn!"

"Exactly. And only an experienced sorcerer could conjure up a vast magic circle. It would have to be huge to contain all the people in the city."

"And then everyone could escape without being in any danger," added Jade.

"Not quite. The enchantment would not last longer than

ten minutes, which barely leaves us enough time to open the gates of the city and flee. But to reach the border of the dukedom of Divulyon, we'd have to renew the spell several times. And that's the insurmountable problem: it's already exhausting enough to use such powerful magic, but casting the same spell repeatedly in such a short time is almost impossible."

"*Almost,*" said Jade meaningfully. "Therein lies the difference."

Suddenly, Opal spoke up.

"Adrien, you said you haven't found a sorcerer who can carry out your plan?"

"That's right," confessed the young man.

"*We* could do it—well, I think we could," she said.

"Us? How?" asked Amber.

"The Stones!" replied Opal. "Since we need a source of powerful magic . . ."

Adrien didn't bother to feign amazement at Opal's words, because he had been waiting for just such a moment to arise.

"Let's suppose that this is possible," he said. "There's still a second problem. We also have to let everyone in Nathyrnn know exactly when the escape is going to happen, so that they'll be ready."

Adrien knew that the revolt could not succeed without some bloodshed, but he did not want to frighten his new allies unnecessarily.

"When will the escape take place?" asked Amber.

"Let's say, in one month."

He watched for Jade's reaction. It was the one he had hoped for.

"No!" protested Jade. "I'm not going to wait a month. I want to reach Fairytale as soon as we can."

"What do you mean by 'as soon as we can'?" asked Amber uneasily.

"Tonight."

"Tonight?" cried Amber and Adrien in unison.

"It should be possible," replied Jade. "Our enemies contacted Opal using telepathy. Let's use this same method to alert the people of Nathyrnn!"

"To reach every mind in the city," began Adrien, "we'd have to—"

"We'd have to try!" interrupted Jade. "If we let ourselves be held back by doubt, we'll stay in this place for ever, and that is out of the question!"

"It's not that simple," warned Adrien. "It will take a huge effort. . . . Oh, well—you're right. If you've managed to get in here, you'll manage to get us out of here!"

he concluded, carried away by Jade's enthusiasm.

Amber took a deep breath. She wasn't completely convinced, but Jade and Opal had already taken their Stones out of their black velvet purses. Amber hesitated, wondering whether the trust they placed in Adrien had been a bit premature; after all, they had only just met him. But she took out her Stone anyway. Actually, the prospect of remaining imprisoned in Nathyrnn didn't thrill her any more than it did Jade.

"Just concentrate on your objective: to warn the citizens about the escape," said Adrien. "If your message is clear enough, and your will strong enough, people will be convinced. Concentrate all your strength on that."

Opal nodded in assent, but Amber grew tense without knowing why. Holding tight to their Stones, the three girls focused their thoughts on liberating Nathyrnn. They had no idea how deeply they were concentrating, and their cheeks flushed with the effort. Then something completely unexpected happened. The girls closed their eyes simultaneously, and before Adrien's astonished gaze, out of nowhere a translucent sphere materialized around them and began to rise into the air, while the girls floated lightly inside. The sphere seemed as fragile as a bubble about to burst, but in reality it was more solid than metal armor. The girls themselves noticed nothing. An image had come to them of a crowd streaming out of the city gates. The girls murmured words they did not know, saw visions they did not understand. Something had possessed them, and yet this something seemed to come from their innermost being. Without knowing it, they were sending these thoughts to the entire population of Nathyrnn.

Impressed, Adrien watched the scene unfolding before him. He heard the words that Jade, Opal, and Amber were emitting telepathically, and was certain the inhabitants of Nathyrnn would now join the revolt—such was the persuasiveness of the girls' voices echoing in his mind.

After a quarter of an hour, the sphere containing the three girls slowly descended and landed on the ground, vanishing as suddenly as it had appeared.

Jade and Opal did not seem at all affected by the miracle they had just performed, and quietly returned to their chairs. Jade smiled, proud of herself, but Amber's eyes had a vacant look. She sat down heavily on the floor and began to cry.

"Never . . . I'll never see her again. . . . I never should have . . . and without a word of apology . . . I won't survive. . . ." Then, abruptly, her tone changed, and she shook her fist threateningly. "I don't want to!" she shouted violently. "No! I want to be free! Stop!"

"Amber!" cried Jade. "What's going on?"

Adrien sighed and said, "This can occasionally happen, although I assumed with your powers you would be immune to it. In making contact with every single inhabitant of the city, Amber has absorbed all their thoughts. She will have to experience each person's emotions before she can get rid of them. It will take several hours."

"Why didn't it happen to Opal and me?" asked Jade.

"Amber must be very sensitive," explained Adrien. "But don't worry. She'll come out of it, and she'll just be left with a few bad memories."

"You're sure?" said Jade.

"Absolutely. The most important thing is, you succeeded! It's quite a feat, and it means that we have a real chance. Well done!"

"Thank you," said Jade smugly. "That wasn't so hard."

"So much the better. What's ahead of us will be."

"We'll see," said Jade, and added rather loftily, "I'm not afraid."

Paris: Present Day

I woke up: after what seemed like an eternity, I had finally emerged from my deathlike slumber. For the first time in a long while I could hear my heart beating; I felt alive, and happy that I was. I could just make out, barely visible, a glimmer of light at the end of this black tunnel of pain and sorrow, this hopeless daily gloom.

Before that night, I had not been able to forget that death was stalking me, and would snatch me away without pity. I was frightened. I was cold. My life had no meaning. I wasn't dead, but might just as well have been. The days were all alike: desperate, useless, and filled with suffering. My disease was eating away at me. I couldn't take it anymore. I had run out of tears, and courage; I had nothing left. Everything had turned out to be in vain. In the end, my existence had been reduced to nothing, and I hadn't even enough strength left to see the injustice of my own despair.

Just another night, exactly the same as those that had preceded it and those that would follow. At least I had thought so as I drifted off to sleep. Usually, I never dreamed. I slept very little, and badly. But that night something extraordinary happened. I had a fantastic dream—about an unbelievable reality. I had the feeling that somewhere, in a distant world, the dream was being lived out. How could I be sure that dreams weren't actually messages from some other real existence, while my senseless life was in fact just the imaginary reflection of that unknown world?

I was overcome by a fit of coughing. The dream—I clung to it as hard as I could, with every thought. Jade, Opal, and Amber . . . Strange! The initials of their names formed my nickname, Joa. Before, everyone had always called me that; it is short for my real name, Joanna. I tried to swallow the lump in my throat. I had thought I was through with the time when tears of longing and regret would well up in my eyes without warning. That belonged to the past. Over and done with. From now on, I had no name anymore, because no one bothered to talk to me. I was nothing, just a body, almost motionless, on a bed in a room. Nothing.

I closed my aching eyes. Hope would get me nowhere. But I would go on dreaming.

11

REBELLION!

JADE AND ADRIEN HAD PREPARED A DETAILED escape plan and were convinced it would succeed. After feverishly searching for a particular magic formula in the few books of sorcery hidden in the city, the young man had at last waved in triumph a yellowed sheet of ancient, crumbling paper, which Jade had examined. Together they had agreed on their plan of action. Now the time had come to cast the spell.

"It's too late to go back," thought Opal. She would have to go through with it. And yet something inside her kept trying to persuade her otherwise.

Amber had emerged from her torpor, but still felt weak. Jade and Adrien were anxious to begin.

Jade picked up the formula. Opal went over to her. Still feeling dizzy and a little muddled, Amber joined them.

"Right," said Adrien, his heart pounding, "this is it. You have to recite the formula over and over, without stopping. The magic circle is invisible. The magic will draw strength from your own energy."

The three girls took out their Stones.

"If all is well," continued Adrien tensely, "the people of Nathyrnn should be gathering at this moment before the city gate. I will go and join them. While you recite the formula, I will open the gate. Then you will join me, and everyone will be freed."

"We know," said Jade. "It's simple."

"It will be hard for you to walk," warned Adrien. "You'll surely be greatly weakened by the strength of the spell. Let's hope the exhaustion doesn't hit you until after we leave Nathyrnn."

"No problem," Jade cut in impatiently.

"Remember to concentrate," continued Adrien, ignoring her.

"Yes, yes, you've already explained everything to us," grumbled Jade.

There was no more time for talking. Adrien left to join the inhabitants of Nathyrnn. The three girls held their Stones and began to recite the magic formula. Nothing happened. The words didn't make any sense at all. They read the formula over again and again. Then suddenly they began to feel the weariness Adrien had warned them about. After a few minutes, realizing that the spell had been cast successfully, they all stopped at the same time. They weren't physically tired, but they were no longer able to think or speak; they had become mindless bodies. And yet, as if controlled by an unknown power, they knew what they had to do. They rushed to the entrance to the city, where they found Adrien waiting by the open gate. The people of Nathyrnn were overjoyed at the prospect of regaining their freedom.

"There you are!" exclaimed Adrien when he caught sight of the three girls. "Everything seems to have gone smoothly. Now we have to evacuate everyone; some will come to Fairytale with us, while others will go back to their place of birth."

Jean Losserand was among that last group. He was finally going to see his old mother again, and his real home. In the throng of people hurrying to leave, he waved to Jade, Opal, and Amber with tears of happiness and disbelief in his eyes, but the girls didn't see him: he was unrecognizable in his newfound joy.

"You're going to have to press on without me," Adrien told the girls. "I must release the prisoners from their cells. I know where the keys are, but I'll have to move quickly. Go toward Fairytale for about ten minutes, then stop to rest and wait for me."

Without a word, the girls left the city, following the crowd returning to Fairytale. Their minds were still blank, and they showed no surprise at the unbelievable scene: the entire population of Nathyrnn was streaming through the city gate, while the Knights of the Order were spellbound in sleep.

The girls and some of the rejoicing crowd marched together into the darkness; after ten minutes, they stopped, following Adrien's instructions. A few moments later, the spell was broken, and the three girls fainted. The magic had sapped all their strength: while the spell was working, the girls had been sustained by its power, but now they were completely drained, and could not be roused from their torpor.

Some ten minutes later, Adrien arrived at the head of more than a hundred and fifty prisoners.

"For the moment, everything's going fantastically well," he exulted.

Then someone showed him the three girls laid out unconscious on the bare ground. Adrien knew that their condition wasn't serious, but when he saw Jade lying sense-less and unmoving, he felt a pang.

"We're continuing on," he announced. "I'll carry one of the girls, and two of you will take the others. They must awaken before we reach the border. These are the girls who cast the spell, and it's thanks to them that we've got this far."

The crowd murmured in astonishment. Adrien waved for silence.

"They will not be strong enough to cast another spell and put the knights who guard the border to sleep. We have no choice: we'll have to prove that our dreams are worth living for, that our courage is not an illusion. We will have to fight."

A clamor of fear went up, but Adrien remained calm.

"Each prisoner has taken the sword from a knight in Nathyrnn. Since some prisoners are too young or too weak to fight, their weapons will be given to the most valiant among us. We have not escaped in vain! We have one goal, and it is close. Let those courageous enough to fight step forward. Hope is invincible!"

The border of the dukedom of Divulyon was very well guarded, but Adrien's passion and unshakable will inspired every sturdy, brave man to come forward. Adrien took charge of handing out the weapons.

"Hope is invincible," he repeated softly, as if trying to convince himself.

The people of Nathyrnn set out for the border again.

Two men had picked up Jade and Amber, so Adrien found himself carrying Opal. The young man noticed that there was a nobility about her, and as he held her in his arms, he became aware of the warmth of her body. Looking around him, Adrien noted the fierce determination shining in everyone's eyes: women, children, old men, all were pressing forward bravely. It was a dark night, but the hard and rocky road they were taking was the path to freedom. The crowd was quiet, savoring the fleeting tranquility all around them.

Soon Jade, Opal, and Amber regained consciousness. They felt sore, quite feeble, and their heads ached, but their minds were clear. They walked unsteadily and had to be helped along for quite a while. Realizing the gravity of the situation, they tried to cast a new spell, but they were too weak, and their efforts failed.

In about a quarter of an hour, the troop reached the border of the dukedom of Divulyon. The darkness concealed them from their enemies, who stood before them in the hundreds: the Knights of the Order. And behind them lay the magnetic field, forming a dome over Fairytale. Although the field was opaque, it gave off a dazzling light.

"Fight fiercely," Adrien urged his armed men. "Create a diversion so that the weakest among us may cross first, and don't fall back until we are the last ones left. Stir up as much trouble as you can."

With these words, he ran forward brandishing his sword, followed by every man fit enough to do battle. Some had no weapons and went into combat barehanded, shouting valiantly.

At first they had the advantage of surprise. As mothers and their children ran helter-skelter toward the magnetic field, the Knights of the Order, busy defending themselves against the attack, were able to stop only a few of them. The children entered Fairytale without any difficulty, and their mothers managed to follow them. But on the battlefield the attack quickly turned into a disaster. The Knights of the Order triumphed easily over their adversaries; only about a dozen men, including Adrien, were really able to challenge them. Many of the former inhabitants of Nathyrnn now lay gravely wounded or dying. Hanging back in the darkness there remained only a handful of frail youths, some frightened old men, many middle-aged women, and Jade, Opal, and Amber.

"If we wait, we won't get through," said Jade urgently. "We have to try our luck now and take advantage of the enemy's confusion. Run! Save yourselves! Don't stop—dash in between the ranks. There's still some hope left, so run for it!"

Gathering up what little strength she had regained, Jade rushed fearlessly toward the battlefield, where she seized the sword of a man lying on the ground in a pool of blood. Her thorough education had included training in the arts of war. Drawing on her knowledge, Jade raised the sword. At that moment, the din of clashing arms died down, then ceased altogether. Both the Knights of the Order and the fugitives could not help but be struck by the sight of the proud fourteen-year-old girl with raven-black hair. Her image seemed completely out of place on that blood-soaked field. Uncertain how to react, the Knights of the Order hesitated. This was a mistake. Jade, swift and agile, sprang to the attack. Amber, Opal, and the other unarmed fugitives then hurried toward the magnetic field. Amber passed through it easily, while a few others, after encouraging one another nervously, managed to follow her, but most of them, including Opal, were unable to cross into Fairytale.

Suddenly, Adrien, who was fighting passionately, shouted to Jade and the last men who remained, "We must fall back! If we don't, we won't survive!"

But Jade didn't listen to him. Such was her prowess that she was triumphing over the most experienced Knights of the Order.

"Jade! Come on! There are too few of us—we cannot win!"

Almost with regret, Jade retreated toward the magnetic field with Adrien and the other men. Hastily grabbing her Stone, she tried to cross the barrier of Fairytale. "I believe in it," she told herself, "and I must go and see Oonagh. Fairytale exists—and the impossible as well." She felt a tremendous pain as she hit the magnetic field: her entire body was violently repulsed. An icy wind blew through her. She tried to advance, but could not. Then she clenched her fists and closed her eyes, and when she opened them again, she understood that she had passed into Fairytale.

On the other side of the magnetic field, things were going very badly. The few surviving combatants had crossed the barrier after Jade, leaving on the other side only Adrien and those who could not manage to believe in the impossible, with Opal among them. Realizing that their opponents were fleeing the battlefield, the Knights of the Order began to pursue them. Some of the last fugitives were weeping in despair, others shrieking in terror, and Adrien could not bring himself to abandon them.

"All you need to do is believe," Adrien pleaded. "Just try, remember a childhood dream, it doesn't matter which one. You'll get through. . . ." But he knew his words were useless and that it was too late. Then something staggering happened: Opal walked out to meet the approaching enemy.

"Knights!" she called out in a firm, strong voice. "I do not ask you to spare me. But be compassionate enough to judge my companions fairly. Their only crime has been to seek their freedom. Do they really deserve to die?"

Adrien stared at Opal in admiration. She, whose eyes were always modestly downcast, was gazing unflinchingly at the enemy. She held herself with such majesty, and looked, at that moment, invincible. And she was so beautiful. . . . Adrien realized that he'd been blind. He loved Opal. He ran toward her to protect her, to tell her how he felt, but a Knight of the Order was faster than he was. The knight had sneered at Opal's words, which carried no meaning for him; he had been taught to take lives, not to save them. He drew his keen sword and with a brutal smile, plunged it pitilessly into Opal's heart.

Adrien arrived only in time to catch Opal's lifeless body in his arms. As he held her, his garments stained with her scarlet blood, he thought she had never looked so beautiful, serene even in death. With tears in his eyes, he pressed his lips to Opal's still warm, soft mouth.

"I loved her," he said simply.

The Knights of the Order looked at one another. They were used to weeping and lamentation, to shouts of accusation—none of that could touch their hearts anymore. Enough: it was time to get the job done.

But Adrien continued, in a sad, steady voice that did not seem to belong to him: "It's not your fault."

The knights stiffened in surprise.

"You were trained to fight and to kill. It's your job, and you do it well. You are men who know how to bear arms better than anyone else."

The knights grew more and more astonished.

Quietly, Adrien took Opal's Stone from its black velvet purse and held it tightly, as she had done before.

"And yet," he continued, "you have forgotten the most important thing. You all have hearts; you can feel love. And that is what makes you real men."

His audience nodded slowly and, strangely enough, not one of them ventured to raise his sword again.

"You have killed the one I loved," said Adrien, "but I do not reproach you for it."

Was it Adrien's words that moved the knights, or the vision of the young man bearing Opal's dead body? Or did the Stone release some kind of magic? No one would ever know.

Then Adrien said with great dignity, "If you are men, you know what you must do now."

And a Knight of the Order, hesitantly, sheathed his sword. The others followed his example. They were not sure they had chosen correctly, but something deep inside them had impelled them to make this decision.

Turning his back to them, Adrien walked toward the magnetic field. He held tight to the Stone, choking back tears. He was now one with Opal. She had loved him. He loved her.

He passed easily through the magnetic field of Fairytale. Although hope had failed, love had triumphed over the impossible.

12

THE NAMELESS ONE

THE WOUND WAS DEEP: A BLOODY GASH ON HIS left forearm. The day before, he'd had to fight off the Bumblinks, wicked creatures who were rife in the northern forest of Fairytale. He had tried to travel through the woods instead of spending long, arduous days going around them, a decision he now regretted. The forest was teeming with evil spirits who resented any human presence. In just the last three days he had already fought two battles, and his horse had been killed in one of them. Luckily, night was falling, and the inhabitants of the forest were settling down to sleep.

He had halted in one of the few clearings, and he felt completely drained. Suddenly he heard a sound, and with his good hand, swiftly drew his gleaming sword. A form appeared. The young man waited, on his guard. The stranger drew near: short, stocky, he wore an ample dark green tunic and at his waist, a sword. It was impossible to tell his exact age, for although a few lines furrowed his brow, his expression was still youthful. An unruly shock of light blond hair fell over his forehead. His nose was small and flat, his lips pale but full. His eyebrows, like his hair, were fine and almost white, while his large, dark eyes seemed merry, yet at the same time wise with experience. Although he was smiling broadly and seemed friendly, something about him hinted that he could prove a formidable foe if the situation demanded it. Was he human? At first glance, his appearance was very much that of a man. But on closer inspection his skin revealed a slight silvery sheen.

"Sheathe your sword, stranger!" cried the creature. "My intentions are peaceful."

The young man with the wounded arm hesitated at first, unconvinced, but after a moment's reflection he complied with the creature's request and put away his weapon.

"I've traveled a long way to find you," continued the newcomer. "My name is Elfohrys, and I've come not to fight you, but to seek your help."

Elfohrys stepped closer and studied the young man before him: he was about eighteen years old, with dark brown hair and deep blue eyes flecked with emerald green. His face was grave, and his intense gaze was imbued with melancholy.

Elfohrys caught his breath: "At last," he told himself.

"Tell me," he asked, "aren't you a hovalyn, or a knight errant, as the common folk say?"

"I am," confirmed the young man.

"And what is your name? You may tell me, have no fear," Elfohrys assured him, in mounting excitement.

"I have no name," confessed the young hovalyn. "Or at least, not that I know of. Two years ago, I awoke in a field without any memory of my past. I decided to become a knight errant and go in search of my real name."

"The Nameless One!" exclaimed Elfohrys admiringly. "Your reputation is known throughout all Fairytale! Everywhere, people speak of a gallant hovalyn seeking his own name. Are you truly the Nameless One?"

"Unhappily, yes. My quest seems to have led me nowhere."

"It is within my power to assist you. I can help you travel through this forest, and will accompany you even farther on your way."

"But why should you wish to help me?"

"I, too, am on a quest, but I may not reveal to you either its purpose or my destination." I am seeking the Chosen One, added Elfohrys to himself, and I believe I have found him.

The hovalyn asked no questions; after all, he welcomed

a traveling companion, even a mysterious one. The silent young man's thoughts turned, as always, toward his dream: to have an identity. He had wandered in vain through most of Fairytale asking everyone if they knew anything about him. En route he had fought many monsters that had been terrorizing the population, and admittedly he had been richly rewarded, but glory was not what he wanted. At night, after having faced a thousand perils, he never fell asleep without wondering what his name was and where he had come from. He had invented hundreds of pasts for himself, depending on his moods; but this brought him little comfort, and frustration continued to eat away at him as he wandered on his fruitless mission.

It was growing late, and he was getting hungry. The youth opened his heavy leather bag and took out some bread, a gourd of water, some smoked turkey, and a strange-looking fruit. He offered to share his food with Elfohrys, who declined politely, producing an extraordinary-looking meal from his own bag: a sticky purple mass, which he devoured. Quickly satisfied, he waited patiently while his companion ate his own repast. Without a word, the Nameless One made a crackling fire, and sat down beside it to ponder his unexpected situation. All of a sudden he had found himself in the company of a stranger about whom he knew absolutely—or almost—nothing. Could he trust him?

Elfohrys had stretched out and was already fast asleep.

The young hovalyn could not manage sleep himself and lay staring up at the twinkling stars. He tried to recognize the different constellations and remember their names. He was overcome with anguish . . . What was he? Who was he? Nothing but a body, a soul in pain, with no memory, nothing that would make him a human being. He was a stranger even to himself. He drew his sword from its scabbard and studied its long, glossy blade, so smooth and sharp. He imagined the blade piercing his own heart. Would he feel cold? Perhaps not; he already carried winter inside him, an eternal winter of questions without answers. Of what use was he in this world?

The stars shone more brightly than usual. He got up, sword still in hand, and began to walk without knowing where he was going, without worrying that he might become lost. What did it matter? He took a winding path and plunged into the darkness. He walked on and on without stopping, oblivious to his surroundings, arriving at last in a moonlit clearing. Spying a lake, he went to its edge and sat contemplating his face in its clear water. This face of his—what did it represent if he did not have a name? Alone with his thoughts, he sat there for a long time, his sword lying by his side. Suddenly, his reflection was disturbed, and from the lake rose a beautiful creature like a mermaid, with a woman's body and two tails of equal size covered in golden scales. Her features were delicate, her blue eyes glinted with gold, and her skin was almost too white, too flawless. Her black hair, tumbling in heavy, silken curls to her shoulders, did not seem wet from the waters of the lake from which she had just emerged. In her slender hands she held a golden casket encrusted with pearls.

"Mortal!" she said fearlessly. "You have dared to approach the Lake of Torments! Only those who suffer may gaze at their reflection in its waters; all others drown themselves, having sought here a consolation they did not deserve. My sisters and I are the guardians and mistresses of the lake. We show ourselves rarely, and only to those worthy of us. I have come to speak to you, mortal, for I must give you something that belongs to you."

"You are mistaken. I possess only my body, my soul— nothing else belongs to me. . . . I am nothing, and do not even have a name. I am called the Nameless One."

"I know your identity, your past, and even some of your future. There are many who know as much as I do, without knowing you. But even if you were to ask me, I would not reveal to you the name you received at birth, for that is not my mission. The only thing I have the right to give you is this casket. It was entrusted to us, to my sisters and me, many years ago, and we promised to give it to a particular person, destined to appear at this lake one day. That person is you, mortal. Those who entrusted the casket to us had one wish: that you guard its contents carefully."

The Nameless One seized the object. Without a sound, the mermaid with the jet-black locks sank back into the depths of the lake. Dumbfounded, but curious, the young man slowly opened the casket, holding his breath, his heart pounding wildly.

In an instant he snapped it shut violently, his intense disappointment shaking him to the core.

The casket was empty.

The Thirteenth Councilor did not often fly into a rage. This time, however, he was in an indescribable fury; he was shaking, and his features were distorted with anger. When he shouted, his voice echoed through the rooms of the palace of the Council of Twelve.

"What?" he roared. "You tell me that all the inhabitants of Nathyrnn have escaped? Do you take me for an imbecile?"

The image of a Knight of the Order, quaking with fright, appeared on a large, thin plaque of gold floating in the air.

"Uh . . . Yes, everyone has escaped," confessed the man in a voice that was barely audible.

"And how do you explain that?" bellowed the Thirteenth Councilor. "Are you going to tell me, perhaps, that you just happened to be asleep when they escaped?"

"Well, actually—yes," stammered the Knight of the Order, confused and ashamed.

"You dare to lie to me? Do you not know the fate that awaits you? Death! And dishonor! In the public square!"

"But I assure you, I am not lying."

"Give me the border of the dukedom of Divulyon—at once!"

The image faded instantly, replaced by the face of another Knight of the Order.

"Commander-in-Chief of the Knights of the Order guarding the border of Divulyon, at your service!" he barked.

"Commander," snarled the Thirteenth Councilor, beside himself with rage, "did you arrest a large number of fugitives a few hours ago?"

"The thing is . . ." replied the commander, suddenly humble and hesitant.

"What happened?" cried the councilor. "Don't lie to me!"

"We did in fact intercept a number of people. We neutralized most of them. We fought valiantly. Our troops were hard pressed. We—"

"I want to know if anyone crossed into Fairytale!"

"Yes," admitted the knight miserably.

"But that's impossible!" shrieked the Thirteenth Councilor. "Who was leading this revolt?"

"Apparently, a young man we have not been able to identify."

"Were there three girls, about fourteen years old?"

"I believe so. One of them in particular was an extremely fine warrior."

"Don't tell me she's dead, or you'll meet the same fate!"

"No, not her. A different one."

"Which one? Describe her!"

"Blond, milky skin, pale eyes, simple clothing . . ."

"What? You've just signed your own death warrant, knight!"

With a wave of his hand, the Thirteenth Councilor made the golden plaque vanish. He clenched his fists furiously—all had not gone according to plan. If he had managed to prevent the girls from reaching Fairytale he could have destroyed them quickly. Now Jade and

Amber were beyond his reach . . . for the time being.

It was time for a new plan. True, Opal had died too soon for his liking, but together, the Stones were a threat, they were powerful. Without Opal, the other two were vulnerable—and he would show them no mercy.

Before long, the Prophecy would be nothing but a waste of paper, a meaningless book. At that thought, his face twisted terrifyingly into a grimace of joy.

13

DEATH

THE COUNTRYSIDE WAS SHROUDED IN DARKNESS, but they could vaguely discern wooded hills and plains of dense, wild grasses.

The former inhabitants of Nathyrnn hugged one another joyfully, their faces transformed by happiness. How could they not believe in the impossible after seeing the merciless Knights of the Order sheathing their swords?

Speechless with sorrow, only Adrien, Jade, and Amber did not share in the general euphoria. Opal's death had shocked and overwhelmed them. She was gone, never to return, and she had left them so suddenly that they could not quite believe it, although Adrien held her lifeless body in his arms. Her blond curls tumbled in the breeze, a thin smile was frozen on her pale lips, and her face had a waxen pallor. In spite of everything, even in death, she was still beautiful, and seemed all the more untouchable.

Adrien held back his tears and put on a brave face to

hide his grief and bitter regret. Still carrying his sad burden, he led Jade and Amber to a modest but handsome
manor, the home of his friend Owen of Yrdahl. The front
door to the manor always stood open in welcome, so
Adrien simply made his way through dark corridors to a
guest room he had often used, paying no attention to the
few late-night revelers, who looked at him curiously.

When he reached the room, he laid Opal down gently
on the clean white sheets of the bed, knelt in front of
her, took her still-warm hand in his, and gazed at her in
silence.

Standing slightly behind him, Jade and Amber no longer
knew what was happening, where they were, or what they
were doing. They couldn't think, let alone move. They
could not grasp that Opal was dead.

Amber couldn't help crying. Blinded by tears, she
wondered why life was so incomprehensible and why it
relentlessly pursued those whom it had decided to
destroy. She had thought that nothing could touch Opal,
that she was in some way immortal. Why had Opal disappeared in such a cruel and untimely way?

Jade felt bad: she hadn't been able to feel real sorrow at
Opal's fate. She had shed a few tears, but they'd been
inspired more by her horror of death itself, by her dread of

plunging one day into an endless void, of not being able to think and dream, of being erased from the world, forgotten. A little ashamed, Jade admitted to herself that she had absolutely detested Opal. Even now that she was dead, Jade couldn't summon any affection for her, only a hint of compassion. Jade was aware, however, that she, Opal, and Amber had belonged together in some vague way, forming a whole that should not have been wrenched apart. Opal was not supposed to have died, she was certain of that. Her feelings were in turmoil: she wasn't really sorry that Opal had died, but she felt guilty because of her callousness. She remembered the dead girl's chilly disdain for her, but a voice reproached her for being hardhearted and arrogant, reminding her that Opal had been vital to their quest.

Just then a man entered the room. Well built, with broad shoulders, he was simply dressed and seemed about twenty years old. He had a frank and engaging smile and appeared to be beside himself with happiness.

"Adrien!" he shouted. "You've come back! I jumped right out of bed when I learned you were here! Tell me, who are these charming ladies?" Turning to Jade and Amber, he announced, "Let me introduce myself: I am Owen of Yrdahl, an old friend of Adrien's, and I'm delighted to meet you! Welcome to my home!"

Adrien rose, and now Opal's body could be seen lying on the bed.

"Look, Owen! She's dead! Dead! It's my fault. A Knight of the Order murdered her, but I could have stopped him! And I did nothing. . . ."

Owen's smile vanished instantly. He rushed to Opal's side, seized her wrist, and looked at the blood still flowing from her wound. Then he dashed from the room without a word. Jade and Amber stared at each other in astonishment. A few minutes later, Owen of Yrdahl returned with a short, stout, middle-aged man who examined Opal without a word.

"This is Lloghin," explained Owen, "one of our most experienced healers. Of course your friend's case is not really serious, Adrien, but it would be better if she didn't lose too much blood."

"Owen," replied Adrien miserably, "don't make fun of me! Opal is dead, and I don't see how a healer can change that! It's not something to joke about."

"Joke?" Then Owen hit his forehead and cried, "That's right, you haven't heard!"

"Heard what?" asked Adrien, who felt an insane glimmer of hope return to his heart.

"Death is on strike! She hasn't done for two

centuries, and it's very annoying. Your friend is alive."

"Very annoying?" repeated Amber. "I don't see what's so annoying about a miracle! What is Death on strike for?"

"Everyone knows that Death lives in Fairytale—in an inaccessible area, obviously. And just a few hours ago, she decided to stop working. So, for now, no one can die."

Jade and Amber were stunned. Adrien, who was used to Fairytale, could only weep tears of relief.

"Death is depressed," continued Owen. "She claims that no one loves her, which is true, naturally. But she would like to be appreciated for her true worth. They say she wants to kill herself. Since that's impossible, she's become even more depressed. Her advisers are at their wits' end."

"So Opal is alive!" rejoiced Amber.

"Yes, but it will be some time before she is completely well again. That's why we must stop the flow of blood."

Lloghin the healer was now applying balms and compresses to Opal's wound as he chanted strange words over her.

"The last time Death went on strike there were terrible consequences," continued Owen. "The strike lasted about ten years. People who hurt themselves or became ill during that time got rapidly better, but those who had already been sick or injured continued to linger in that state with no hope of deliverance through Death. In the end, her advisers managed to make her see reason, but I have the impression that this time, it's more serious."

"What a story!" marveled Amber.

"Now that your worries about your friend—Opal, is that right?—have been put to rest, perhaps we might be introduced to one another?"

"Well," replied Jade, yawning with fatigue, "we've known Adrien for less than a day, but we did liberate a city with him, and we've come to meet Oonagh, who reads people's hearts or something like that. By the way, I'm Jade, but that's all I can tell you about myself, except that I was driven from my palace by my own father and I have enemies everywhere, which isn't my idea of a nice life, but what can you do. . . ?"

"I'm Amber," said Amber simply.

"Jade, Opal, Amber," murmured Owen, as if struck by an obvious thought.

Jade yawned again. She was so exhausted she no longer knew what she was saying.

"Sleep," she mumbled, feeling her eyelids growing heavier and heavier.

"Ah—yes, of course, I'll show you girls to a bedroom,"

said Owen, adding to Adrien, "Wait here for a few minutes—I'll be back."

When he returned, Owen was bursting with excitement.

"The Stones of the Prophecy! You've brought the girls everyone in Fairytale is talking about! You owe me an explanation!"

"They're unbelievable girls," said Adrien, "and don't hold it against Jade if she was asleep on her feet. A little while ago, she fought the Knights of the Order."

"But it's so rash of her to reveal her name and her story—doesn't she realize the risk she's running?"

"No, I don't think she does," replied Adrien. "She doesn't seem to know much about the Prophecy."

"Then it's not for us to enlighten her. Now, tell me what the Outside is like!"

"It's so different from here," sighed Adrien. "You just can't imagine—the two worlds are almost complete opposites. Outside is huge, beautiful, just as you've heard on this side, but it's also hard, violent, and primitive. Life there is rough and archaic. The people don't know what freedom is; they live in an unjust and class-ridden society."

"You must be exaggerating."

"Maybe . . . no, I don't think so. How about you, tell me: what has changed over here?"

Owen's face grew solemn.

"We've begun to despair," he confided in a low voice.

"No . . . Don't tell me that . . . the Chosen One . . ."

"Yes. He still hasn't been found."

"This is getting serious. According to the Prophecy, it won't be long now until the battle. And if the Chosen One hasn't turned up, how will we fight? The army will begin to assemble soon, but without him, it won't help us at all."

"That's what everyone is worried about," said Owen glumly. "They're losing heart. Oonagh is waiting, but nothing is happening. The Chosen One has not revealed himself."

"And if he doesn't come?"

"That will mean that Néophileus was wrong, that the Prophecy is false, and that our hopes are in vain," Owen finished with a sigh. "But that can't be possible!"

"If the Chosen One doesn't exist, then perhaps the Stones don't have the power they are supposed to possess."

"And all will be lost," concluded Owen grimly.

14

THE GHIBDULS

THE NAMELESS ONE RETRACED HIS STEPS WITH great difficulty, but dawn found him back in the clearing, lying asleep next to Elfohrys. The forest was bathed in sunshine, clear and bright in spite of the magnetic field around Fairytale. The rustle of leaves in the warm breeze mingled with the day's first notes of birdsong as the forest awoke. The young man and Elfohrys opened their eyes. Stiff and aching, and still drowsy, they were nevertheless determined to be on their way.

Shrill cries sounded in the distance: the inhabitants of the forest were waking as well. Two races shared these woods, the Bumblinks and the Ghibduls.

Elfohrys belonged to a group of magic creatures that were few in number, but much respected, the Clohryuns, a race from which Néophileus himself was descended. The Clohryuns did not possess true supernatural powers, but Elfohrys knew how to defend himself and did not shrink from fighting adversaries more agile than he. A trusted friend had told him of a path leading out of the forest, and even though he had never taken it before, Elfohrys now proposed it to his companion. They would have to be on constant guard, of course, because there was always the risk of encountering some Bumblinks or Ghibduls.

The two travelers set out briskly, with Elfohrys confidently striding along winding paths bordered with brambles and stunted shrubs. The Nameless One felt no fear, for he attached so little importance to his life that he was not afraid of losing it. After a few monotonous hours, Elfohrys left the paths to head into the thick of the forest.

"There's no other way," he told his companion, who simply nodded.

Now the woods seemed even more threatening. The bare, scraggy trees loomed up against a cloudless sky.

"The closer you get to the heart of the forest," explained Elfohrys, "the more you can sense the presence of evil beings. I'm surprised that we've come this far without any trouble."

As time passed and the sun rose higher, the atmosphere became muggy, despite the shade beneath the forest canopy. The young man felt strangely tired and would have liked to stretch out under a tree for a nap. He stared blankly into space and began dragging his feet. Sounds became muffled, and images blurred. He was gasping for breath. Finally all grew dark around him and he collapsed. He heard a reedy voice intoning, "Nothing, nothing, nothing, you are nothing, nothing, nothing. . . ."

Then Elfohrys forced him to listen by sending a pleading telepathic message: "Don't give up, Nameless One! It's a mental attack from the Ghibduls! Wake up, all you need is a little willpower. Don't let them defeat you!"

But Elfohrys's voice irritated the young hovalyn, who wanted to get rid of it. His mouth was dry, and he struggled to tell Elfohrys to be quiet. But instead, without really wanting to, he said clearly, "The casket, in my leather bag!" It was as if someone had put these meaningless words into his mouth. Then he immediately lost consciousness and would gladly have remained in that state for ever.

A few moments later, though, he felt Elfohrys place the pearl-encrusted casket in his hands. Driven by a powerful instinct, he opened it—and was instantly bathed in a refreshing feeling of well-being. He leaped to his feet.

"You've come to!" exclaimed Elfohrys. "I thought you were lost—the Ghibduls' powers of mental persuasion are very strong. I shook you, I shouted, I even used telepathy to help you, but I couldn't rouse you."

"Thank you," said the young man. "If you hadn't been here, I would not have survived."

"Yes, you would have, but the Ghibduls would have captured you and taken you back to their lair to torture you."

"Thank you again," repeated the hovalyn, at a loss for words.

"It was a good thing you mentioned that casket! I found it in your bag, but I just couldn't open it no matter how hard I tried. Tell me, is it enchanted? Does it obey only you?"

"I'm not too sure, I found it along the way. . . ."

Elfohrys let the matter drop, but wondered why his friend had asked for the casket from the depths of his stupor, and how it had managed to save him.

"Nameless One," said Elfohrys abruptly, "when we get out of the forest, where do you plan to go?"

"We aren't out of it yet," replied the young man evasively.

"True, the Ghibduls won't give up easily. You've eluded them, so they'll do everything in their power to take revenge."

"They're formidable enemies," agreed the hovalyn, relieved to see that the conversation was taking a different turn.

But Elfohrys was not so easily put off.

"Be that as it may, you still haven't told me where you're going next."

"I—I was planning on heading for the city of Thaar," came the reluctant reply.

"Thaar?" repeated Elfohrys incredulously. "The City of Origins? How can it possibly interest you, a hovalyn? It's a most dangerous city, very hard to get into, and it has no connection with your quest!"

"I don't know where to go," confessed his companion, "and Thaar is one of the few places I haven't visited yet. It's as simple as that."

"Have you already been to see Oonagh?" asked Elfohrys, hoping he knew what the answer would be.

"No, never. What do you think that creature could tell me? I know only too well what's in my heart: questions, worries, but nothing of my past."

"That's where you're wrong. A long time ago, I went to see Oonagh myself. I learned things I had never suspected, and yet they were written in my heart."

"I'm almost certain her words won't help me at all," insisted the young man. "And anyway, Oonagh lives so far away, in that grotto lost inside a steep mountain. So few people undertake that journey. . . ."

"Trust me. Take my advice: go there. If you don't learn anything about your identity from Oonagh, we'll go to Thaar."

"All right, if it means that much to you, I'll go and see Oonagh," the hovalyn agreed.

Far away, in the very center of the forest, stood the dismal and terrifying lair of the Ghibduls. No one had ever understood them: among themselves they behaved in a manner far superior to that of men, for they never waged war among their own kind, they tolerated one another's faults, and never had family disputes. People mistakenly believed their customs to be backward and their society primitive. The Ghibduls felt love and pity just like any other creatures—perhaps even more so. They lived freely and happily; they made their home in the forest, and never left it. Because of their repulsive appearance, many legends had arisen concerning their cruelty, when in fact they were naturally affectionate and loyal, although fierce in battle. Since they were stronger than other species, they ruthlessly killed any intruders they found, suspecting them of wanting to take over the forest for themselves.

In their eyes, such intruders were savage beasts, a challenging prey doomed to a violent death. The Ghibduls positively enjoyed the feeling of warm blood their hands, and they delighted in its rich, sweet odor. The Ghibduls believed that to die at their hands was a privilege and a blessing for inferior beasts, who were incapable of thinking or loving—which was exactly what those same beasts thought about the Ghibduls.

Now the Ghibduls had just suffered the most stinging insult within living memory: there was a man in the forest, and that man had outwitted them. They had attacked him after his defeat of their friends, the Bumblinks, when he had valiantly defended himself and managed to wound most of his attackers. He wielded an apparently enchanted sword with uncommon skill and, above all, he did not fear death. Until then, the Ghibduls had encountered only men who clung desperately to life. They had been forced to admit that this hovalyn was different, and they had retreated in humiliation. Their pride had been wounded and they were set on taking revenge, but somehow they could not suppress a grudging feeling of admiration for the hovalyn. They had even tried to overthrow him using their mental powers, which they employed only against their most valiant enemies—but the human had triumphed again.

Mortified, the Ghibdul warriors sought counsel with their wise men, the strategists and councilors in charge of matters of the utmost importance. These wise men were themselves taken aback by the warriors' reports, but one of them came up with an astonishingly clever solution. There was violent opposition at first, but the plan eventually won everyone over. The human being who had beaten them had no idea whom he was up against, and the Ghibduls had more surprises in store for him—they could promise him that!

PARIS: PRESENT DAY

I was frightened by the impenetrable, unchanging silence. All I could hear was the constant hum of the machines I was tethered to, that my flickering life was connected to. I had always been scared of the dark. Why pretend otherwise? And to me, that's what death was: complete darkness, eternal and unfathomable. I imagined myself falling into an abyss without anything to hold on to; I saw myself engulfed by nothingness, in a world without feelings, thoughts, colors, lost forever in a void. There would be no more pain. . . . I would dissolve in this emptiness, forget everything, lose everything, every trace of my existence. Actually, if that was what death was, then perhaps I had already left this life. But no, I was still lying here, motionless, pale, trembling convulsively, awaiting the end. I was afraid, so afraid, that I thought my fear might triumph and kill me before my illness could. I had more or less accepted the pain, understood that it would remain until the end, slyly gnawing away at me, but I had never been able to forget this fear always lurking inside me, relentlessly devouring, haunting, and overwhelming me. I was frightened of silence, darkness, time, oblivion, eternity. Death. I wished that I could stop time, order it to halt in its course. I pleaded with it to go backward, to give me back my life, my future. I had nothing left that could help or comfort me. There was only anguish, growing ever worse.

Then the dream had come. It had disrupted my waiting, hurled me outside time, outside the life I'd been leading or the absence of life that was my world. I wanted the dream to go on forever, to make me forget everything else, to wipe it all from the face of the earth. . . . I believed I could live in my dream, making it my reality and turning my sad reality into a distant and impossible dream. Without knowing it, I had timidly begun to hope again. But in the end, it was only a dream, and this grim realization destroyed all my illusions.

Even my dream wouldn't stay with me. I had to face facts: it was just an illusion. So I took a deep breath, and I faced the truth—the one I could see in the furtive glances of the nurses, the desperate truth that hid deep inside me. I could not continue to believe that I could ever have my old life back again: I had neither the right, nor the strength, to hope for that. Joa, always spoiled by her parents, the successful, accomplished girl with so many friends—Joa had ceased to exist.

I reined in my fear; I shattered the shell of fantasy I had tried to construct around myself thanks to that dream. And I said out loud, so I could hear the truth I was trying to escape from: "I'm fourteen years old. And I'm going to die."

15

FAIRYTALE

WHEN SHE WOKE UP, AMBER WAS DISORIENTED and panicked for a moment. Where was she? What had happened? Then the events of the previous day, so charged with emotion, came flooding back to her.

She took her time getting up and had a nice hot bath in a small private room adjoining her own. She sniffed the delicate scents lined up on a shelf and dabbed some perfume behind her ears. Then she dressed, combed her hair, and set off down the corridor outside her bedroom without any idea where she was going. She passed several ornately carved wooden doors without daring to open them, went down many corridors that all looked alike, and finally realized that she was walking around in circles. At last, to her great relief, she met a woman of about fifty, who laughed heartily when Amber explained her dilemma.

"My dear girl," she replied, "this manor isn't big enough for you to get lost in! Come along, follow me, I'll show you the great hall, where you can have a bit of breakfast."

"Actually," said Amber timidly, "I'd like to find Jade, Adrien, and Opal. We arrived together last night. . . ."

The lady's face suddenly looked serious.

"So you're the ones," she said thoughtfully. "Come, I'll take you to your friends."

As Amber followed her, she noticed that the woman was not walking: her body glided along an inch or so above the ground.

"Are you—are you working magic?" she asked awkwardly.

"Magic? That's what I dreamed of as a child, actually, but I couldn't do it. I didn't have the gift."

"But your way of walking without walking . . ." said Amber in confusion.

"That? But my dear girl, I'm a Dohnlusyenne. How else would I get around?"

"Oh, right. Sorry," replied Amber, utterly befuddled.

Just then the Dohnlusyenne opened a door and ushered Amber into a room where she found Adrien at Opal's bedside with Jade and Owen of Yrdahl.

"Amber!" cried Owen. "There you are! How about coming on a ride around Fairytale with us?"

"Wonderful!" she replied eagerly.

"I'm staying behind," announced Adrien. "If Opal

wakes up, I want her to find me right by her side."

Jade, Amber, and Owen left the manor. Three horses were tied up in the courtyard, and as the girls drew closer they noticed subtle differences between these horses and the ones they were used to: these animals had a soft and rather thick brown coat, golden manes that almost seemed to be made of glistening flames, and blue eyes gleaming with intelligence.

"Here are the horses we'll ride," said Owen. "They're real thoroughbreds—you won't find more magical beasts anywhere."

"Magical?" said Amber, disconcerted. "Do they fly, shoot fire from their nostrils, or something like that?"

"Of course not," laughed Owen. "I didn't say that a wizard had enchanted them!"

"Then how are they magical?" asked Amber.

"You're disappointed? If you like, I can give you a more ordinary horse," said Owen with a hint of mischief.

"No, no," said Amber quickly.

They mounted and rode out, Owen leading the way. The two girls were soon puzzled to find there was nothing extraordinary about the landscape of Fairytale: an endless sky of immaculate blue above a few distant peaks crowned with everlasting snows. Amber looked around at the white-capped summits and rolling hills.

"Over there," said Owen, "where those mountains are, that's where Oonagh lives. If you didn't really need to go there, I would advise against it, but, well . . . And never go to the city of Thaar. Don't even try, that's the last thing you should ever do."

"Why?" asked Jade, intrigued by his comments.

"It's more than dangerous," continued Owen. "It's just plain deadly. That city is cursed. They've renamed it again and again, but nothing helps—that city will never change."

"But why?" repeated Jade.

"It doesn't matter," said Owen curtly, suddenly uneasy.

Amber had been only half listening to the conversation; she was stroking her horse's coat, and was surprised to find it rough instead of smooth, as she'd expected.

That reflection had hardly crossed her mind, however, when the texture of the hair changed beneath her finger-tips, becoming silky and pleasant to the touch, exactly as she had imagined it. Curious, she stared down at the animal's coat. White would have been so pretty, she thought—and her wish came true: she saw the horse's coat grow paler until it reached the color she'd had in mind, a dazzling, pure white.

"Owen," cried Amber, "I get it! The horse guesses the

wishes of his rider, and then makes them come true! It's magical. . . ."

"Imagine that!" said Owen teasingly. "Aren't you pleased? These horses have always seemed like excellent mounts to me. . . ."

"They're wonderful!" cried Amber happily. "I just can't believe it, that's all!"

The three young people were traveling along a dull road, past ordinary houses and meadows of no interest, and Amber's suggestion that they run a race was immediately accepted by her companions. Amber concentrated on wanting her horse to gallop as fast as possible—and felt giddy with speed as the wind whipped her face and the ground flew by beneath her horse's hooves. She had never felt anything like it. After a few fantastic minutes, she looked back to see Jade and Owen lagging far behind. She mentally ordered her horse to stop, and waited for her friends.

"I've never seen that before!" exclaimed Owen. "It usually takes a while for the horses to get used to their riders, and long months of training before they will carry out their wishes—and even then the riders must have lots of experience with them. I had to work hard with the horse you're riding before he understood me as well as he does you!"

"Does he have a name?"

"How would I know it? Obviously, he must have one, but naturally a horse never speaks to a person, even if he's able to."

"And you haven't given him a name?" asked Amber.

"No, he wouldn't be pleased, that's not their custom."

"Ah," was all Amber said, because she'd run out of words to express her astonishment.

Since the ride was becoming tiring, the girls readily agreed with Owen's suggestion that they turn back. Jade questioned their host about how the citizens of Fairytale lived.

"We're free," he said simply. "We have responsibilities, of course, but we are all individually responsible for our own actions. We work, we amuse ourselves, we live. . . ."

"But the fairy creatures?" insisted Jade.

"They live among us."

"But then, what's so magical about life here?" asked Jade, who was running out of patience.

"It's just a name, Fairytale—a vague idea, not a way of life. It's a word; it doesn't illustrate reality or try to represent it. And our existence isn't a fairy tale—we all have sorrows, problems, even though we live among magical creatures. . . ." Owen broke off. "Wherever there's life," he said softly, "wherever there are men, there is also evil."

Soon the manor was in sight. The three riders took their horses to a small stable. While Amber fondly admired the stallion she had ridden, a graceful animal whose golden mane stood out against the creamy white of his new coat, his lively blue eyes observed her without a flicker of emotion. Amber left him with regret to follow Owen and Jade.

There was a great disturbance inside the manor, and the three young people had barely set foot inside when a man rushed over to Owen. Jade and Amber recognized him: it was Lloghin, the healer they'd met the night before.

"Something serious has happened," he announced, visibly upset.

"What's wrong? Calm down, Lloghin."

"I can't. . . . A messenger arrived after you left."

"A messenger? The news must have been important!"

"Oh, yes," sighed Lloghin miserably. "Owen, the worst has happened."

"*What* has happened? Tell me!"

"The city of Thaar has fallen."

"What!" shouted Owen of Yrdahl, thunderstruck.

"The messenger is in the great hall," added Lloghin. "I advised him to await your return."

Deeply worried, Owen went off with the healer. The

two girls had no trouble finding the room where Adrien had been watching over Opal, but they stood outside in the corridor for a moment.

"Thaar," murmured Amber thoughtfully. "What's so dangerous about that city? Who has taken it?"

"It's very strange," said Jade. "Owen and the healer look really terrified. And I thought war didn't exist in Fairytale."

"I feel as if I'm living in a dream," mused Amber. "So many things seem unreal to me."

"Well, I've had enough! I want to know what these Stones are, what I am, and why I was chased out of my home," declared Jade. "I want someone to explain to me what the Council of Twelve can possibly have against us. I want to live in a world where things are definite, where I'm not surrounded by mysteries and impossible dreams! As soon as Opal wakes up, we're leaving to go and see Oonagh."

With that, they entered the room to find Opal alone and shaking violently. The two girls rushed over to her. She was still unconscious, but was muttering vague sounds that didn't make any sense. She abruptly fell silent, and lay motionless.

"Where is Adrien?" cried Jade crossly. "He just goes off without any warning, and here we are, with Opal out of her mind, stuck in some manor in the middle of blasted Fairytale!"

"Adrien must have had a good reason to leave the room," replied Amber quietly. "We can go and get Lloghin."

"Where is he? I feel lost here! I'm out of my league, it's all too magical for me!"

"There's nothing magical about the manor," said Amber, "and surely we can manage to find the great hall!"

Suddenly Adrien appeared, wearing a blue-and-gold uniform. He looked particularly determined, but his face was pale.

"Adrien!" cried Jade indignantly. "Where were you?"

"Thaar has fallen," replied the young man.

"Yes, we know," said Amber.

"So there's a war?" asked Jade.

"Yes and no," answered Adrien gravely. He sat down in a wooden chair before continuing. "I'll tell you everything— you ought to know, so that you can tell Opal why I abandoned her."

"You only left while we were riding," said Amber. "It's not such a big deal."

"I don't mean that. I'll be leaving soon. For good."

"But—" interrupted Jade.

"Let me finish, listen to me, both of you. Thaar is not an

ordinary city. Some say that it's haunted by evil. Thaar belongs to the past, and reflects it. Thaar has been called the City of Origins and is the only city that has remained intact for thousands of years, as if it were outside time. This city has never truly been a part of Fairytale and, strangely, even though it lies beneath the magnetic field, Thaar is not protected by it. For a long time the Council of Twelve has been able to reach it through telepathy. That's one of the reasons why this city is so dangerous. There aren't many people living there, and some of them are hungry for power and have betrayed Fairytale by helping the Council of Twelve control the minds of all the inhabitants of Thaar.

"Some citizens did manage to resist, with difficulty, but the dark force of the Council of Twelve has invaded the city and now holds it in its power. From there, the evil could spread throughout Fairytale. The members of the Council of Twelve or even the Knights of the Order can now materialize in the city by using teleportation, thanks to a complex spell that has been cast only a dozen or so times throughout history. It's highly unlikely, however, that they will use this spell. It's almost certain what their plan is: using their minions in Thaar, they will invade the minds of others and enslave or destroy them. And they will succeed in this. Everyone in Thaar has finally stopped resisting. We don't know exactly what's going on there at the moment but, luckily, one of the inhabitants managed to escape. Messengers have been dispatched throughout Fairytale."

"How will everyone fight back?" asked Amber, shivering.

"The plan is simple: regiments of volunteers will encircle the city. If the Council of Twelve tries to take over more of the inhabitants, the soldiers will put up a fight—mentally. In any case, our army will attempt to contact the minds of the inhabitants, to help them, which is almost impossible, given the strength of the Council of Twelve. We will also try to enter the city to fight, to push back the mental attack."

"Wait a minute," said Jade. "Why are you saying 'we'?"

"I've just joined the army," announced Adrien in a voice charged with emotion. "I leave tomorrow."

"You're risking your life?" cried Jade.

"I want to be useful, not to hide shamefully, waiting to see what happens," replied the young man. "They need volunteers. My life or another's, what does it matter?"

"But you'll come back, won't you?" asked Amber.

"Perhaps," said Adrien evasively. "When it's all over. But perhaps not. At least I will have died fighting."

"Adrien, don't be so melodramatic," cried Jade. "You

make it sound as if it's the end of the world!"

The young man gave a faint, strained smile, and said, "I haven't finished. And don't ask me any questions. What I'm going to tell you is very important. Believe me, I'm serious when I say that. . . . I shouldn't say anything, but . . ."

"Oh, just get on with it," snapped Jade.

"You must go and see Oonagh. Now, without delay. We're running out of time."

"What about Opal?" asked Amber.

"Lloghin has given me a potion he has concocted that will bring her round for a few brief moments so that I can say good-bye to her. Then she will fall back into her coma. You'll have to arrange for her to be transported with you. She'll be all right without me."

"But how will we find our way?" asked Amber indignantly, and somewhat fearfully.

"You'll manage. It's crucial. Now, leave me alone with Opal for a few moments. Then you must. Owen will give you the magical horses you rode earlier."

The girls went out into the corridor and closed the door behind them.

"Everybody wants to get rid of us!" fumed Jade. "We're always being chased away!"

Amber said nothing, but Jade was right, and she, too, had had enough.

In the bedroom, Adrien was gazing longingly at Opal. "I'm so sorry," he murmured. From the pocket of his tunic he took out a beautifully carved flask containing what looked like a bubbling blue liquid. As he opened it, a heavy smell of blood, rotting flesh, and death filled the air. Wincing with disgust, the young man held the repulsive mixture close to Opal's nose. When she opened her lips, Adrien poured the miraculous draught into the girl's mouth, and she swallowed it obediently. Slowly, she came around: her nostrils flared; then her lips curved in a smile and she said faintly, her eyes still closed, "I've had such a lovely sleep. . . ." She yawned and opened her eyes.

"Opal!" cried Adrien, his voice thick with emotion.

The girl's vision was still blurred, and it was a moment or two before she came to completely. Then her pale, almost transparent eyes brightened and she breathed softly, "Adrien! You're here. . . . What happened?"

The young man felt tears come to his eyes, but he held them back as he reflected sadly that he was seeing Opal for perhaps the last time.

"I love you," he confessed shakily. "I will always be

thinking of you, until I see you again. I will be near you whenever you think of me."

He could not continue. Her huge eyes fixed on Adrien, Opal seemed overjoyed and miserable at the same time. Sitting up, she flung herself into the young man's arms and whispered, "Don't leave me, don't go, stay with me—it's dangerous, you're risking your life. . . . And I love you."

She tried to say something else, but all at once the light in her eyes died, and she fell back senseless against the pillow.

Adrien never understood how Opal had known that he was going off to fight, but what mattered most to him was the knowledge that she returned his feelings. Now, with love as his shield, he could leave fearlessly to confront the Council of Twelve.

16

GOOD VS. EVIL

AMBER AND JADE MADE THEIR WAY IN SILENCE on horseback toward the snowcapped mountains. They rode past houses, some modest, others imposing, and fields of crops that lined the road. There were only a few laborers, who were singing and laughing merrily instead of cultivating the land. They seemed human, but their long hair looked like spun silver.

Supporting the unconscious Opal as she rode, Jade was wondering where she would sleep that night and what insane adventure she was getting herself into. "Don't laugh," she burst out, "but I get the feeling everybody in the world knows what we're supposed to do—except us! Amber, you know what I've been thinking?"

"No," replied Amber absently.

"If the Council of Twelve is against everyone who knows about Fairytale, it's because it's frightened of them."

"Yes, that seems logical," said Amber.

"Listen, imagine if everyone knew about Fairytale—

there would be rebellions all over the place! Everybody would want to come here. Now, think about it: no one rises up against the Council of Twelve, because no one is brave enough, but it would also be totally useless—there are Knights of the Order everywhere. But, do you know, I bet the main reason no one's doing anything is that most people don't even realize what's going on! You see?"

"Yes," agreed Amber. "The people are deprived of their liberty, their dreams, their ambition. . . . From the moment they're born, they're given a future with no surprises. My parents were peasants, so I was destined to be one too, and I had no choice in the matter. The Council of Twelve robs people of their freedom under the pretext of giving them a stable society, but no one realizes this. They follow the rules without a second thought because they're used to them from birth."

"Before I left home I definitely saw the world only the way I'd been taught to see it. What about you, did you figure this out a long time ago?" asked Jade.

"I always knew it. I grew up freely, on my own, and I took refuge in reading forbidden books and learning about life through them. Look at the world under the Council of Twelve: the sick and weak are considered feeble, useless, and contemptible. People never notice those more unfortunate than themselves—except to make fun of them," Amber replied.

"It's true, people do only what they're ordered to do, they never question anything, they don't give a thought to friendship, affection. . . ." Jade mused. "Anyway, as I was saying, if the Council of Twelve has something against us, that's because it's frightened of us, as unlikely as that may seem. Ever since our births, it's had plenty of time to destroy us, to send Knights of the Order to hunt us down. So if the Council of Twelve is afraid of us now, it must have a very good reason—but I just can't figure out what it could be."

It was now early afternoon and the two girls had not eaten at the manor, so they decided to stop. Before their departure, Owen had given them enough supplies for their entire journey.

Jade and Amber sat down in the cool shade of an oak, and gently laid Opal down beside them. Their companion was still unconscious, but Lloghin had managed to stanch the flow of blood from her wound and it was now healing.

The two girls unpacked their supplies and hungrily attacked the fresh bread, dried meat, and creamy cheese, leaving aside the unfamiliar and less appetizing food.

"You know, Jade," said Amber, "I'm not sorry I came

here, after all. What kind of a future did I have? I didn't really have one at all. I was about to leave childhood behind and see what lay ahead of me: nothing."

"Ye-es," conceded Jade, "but it wasn't the same for me. Only a few days ago I would have proclaimed to the world that I was the daughter of the Duke of Divulyon, I would have told you all about my sumptuous palace, and unlike you, I believed that my future would bring me everything: fame, fortune, whatever my heart desired. Now I feel a little guilty that I didn't know enough to look beyond appearances."

Jade stopped talking and felt her cheeks flush. She would never have imagined that one day she would talk to someone about her feelings! And yet, the Duke of Divulyon had assured her that Opal and Amber would be her enemies, which had turned out to be true for Opal, but not for Amber. Why had he said that? Jade had the unpleasant impression that she had changed since leaving the palace. And Amber was coming dangerously close to being her first friend—a word that had always seemed mysterious to Jade, and yet attractive, too.

No, it wasn't possible! She, Jade, the daughter of the Duke of Divulyon, thinking such things! It was so strange—and she'd only left home a few days ago! She would have sworn that years had passed, perhaps because she sensed that her past was over and done with.

"I've got an idea," said Amber out of the blue. "Why don't we see if we can revive Opal with our Stones?"

"All right, let's try."

Amber took the black velvet purse from Opal's pocket and folded the girl's fingers around the Stone. Then she took out her own amber Stone and squeezed it tight, while Jade did the same with hers. They waited a moment, and then Amber squeezed even harder. The two girls felt that the Stones were trying to reach Opal through their energy, but it was no use: since she was unconscious, it was impossible to reach her the way they had before.

Disappointed, they soon set out on their journey again. Amber took Opal this time, apologizing mentally to her horse for this extra weight. She was sure that her mount understood, even though he didn't answer her.

"I'd really like to give you a name," Amber murmured telepathically, "even though Owen claims you wouldn't like that."

The horse instantly became agitated, and Amber felt a mild discomfort; she guessed that her mount was using telepathy to dissuade her from opposing his wishes.

"Fine, all right, don't get upset! I won't give you a name.

But I wasn't aware that you could communicate feelings and sensations to me. It's astounding!"

The horse stopped. Amber realized that she had annoyed him and wounded his pride.

"I'm sorry! It's just that I'm not used to Fairytale. Many things here are so different from where I come from."

Satisfied with her explanation, the horse walked on.

The girls rode for a long time without knowing whether they were on the right path. They were heading toward the mountains, but were still so far from Oonagh.

Twilight veiled Fairytale in shadows, and then night fell. The travelers weren't tired, but they decided to stop because the countryside seemed more threatening in the dark and the girls were afraid of getting lost or being attacked by an unknown enemy. Adrien had advised them against seeking anyone's hospitality, fearing they might encounter some danger. The girls knew that their enemies could be everywhere. Before, they had felt safe in Fairytale, but now, in the darkness, they didn't know what to think. They sat down under a tree by the side of the road and ate their supper. Then they stretched out on the prickly grass, laying Opal down beside them.

"I've been thinking," said Amber.

"Me, too."

"The inhabitants of Fairytale are believers. They believe in the impossible. They're free. Not necessarily happy, as Owen said, but free to choose their lives. I don't think that war can exist here, in such a peaceful country. In the rest of the world, ruled by the Council of Twelve, people don't believe anymore, they don't dream anymore. They don't know whether they're happy or unhappy. They don't even want to know. There isn't any war out there, either—but there are many things that are forbidden—"

"You're mistaken," cut in Jade. "There's evil here, too— Owen said so. There must have been wars and violence. You can't always live in peace. And over there, on the Outside, war has existed for a long time and still does today. The Council of Twelve fights against freedom and happiness. It won't ever conquer them completely. Wherever there is evil, there must also be goodness. So there is war. There, and here."

"You must be right," replied Amber admiringly. "Good and evil, the eternal battle. . . ."

They both laughed.

"On the Outside," continued Amber, "most people hardly ever think about others. They forget to look around them, they forget about people's feelings. And they don't even realize it! Who would rebel, out there? Who would dare to be different from everyone else? And who would show these others how to change?"

"That's why it's up to Fairytale to help the Outside," concluded Jade. "Here, everyone understands what goes on out there, and they can help them. And we certainly haven't the right to pretend that none of this is happening."

Carried away by her speech, Jade was about to say something else when a faint voice interrupted her, startling both girls.

"Where are we?"

Opal was awake.

"I don't feel well," she said weakly.

Amber crouched down beside her reassuringly. "We're in Fairytale," she explained. "You were hurt, but it isn't serious."

With a stifled cry, Opal touched her wound, which was still painful in spite of Lloghin's expert care.

"Let's get out our Stones," suggested Jade.

Opal and Amber promptly obeyed and, as they all concentrated, they felt a pleasant warmth. For an instant they thought of nothing: they felt relaxed, and their problems melted away. Then the communication slowly faded, and a wave of tiredness enveloped Jade and Amber, as though they had given part of their strength to Opal.

"Thank you. I feel better," sighed Opal. "My wound hardly hurts at all anymore. But I need to rest a little before we set out again. And by the way—where are we going?"

"To see Oonagh, of course," replied Jade tartly.

"But we're in no hurry," added Amber. "Tonight, we'll sleep. Tomorrow, we'll tell you everything."

And the three girls closed their eyes, forgetting all their troubles.

17

THE GHIBDULS' PRISONERS

ELFOHRYS AND THE NAMELESS ONE HAD stopped for the night in a small clearing. There had been no further incidents along the way after the mental attack from the Ghibduls. At one point Elfohrys had become disoriented, but after an hour the two travelers had managed to set out in the right direction again.

Before they lay down to sleep, the young hovalyn had asked how long it would take them to get out of the forest.

"Alas," Elfohrys had replied, "it's not up to me. If we don't run into any more obstacles, perhaps we'll be out of the forest in two days, but it could also take weeks."

After eating and chatting for a little while, they had lain down to sleep. The Nameless One, who'd had almost no rest the night before, had fallen into a deep slumber, unaware that the Ghibduls had been studying him all day long. When they were sure he was asleep, they insidiously entered his mind and numbed it for several hours. They did the same to Elfohrys, so that now even the end of the world would not have disturbed the two companions.

Satisfied, the Ghibdul wise men rubbed their clawlike hands together. Cackling loudly, they sent a dozen warriors to fetch the sleeping travelers back to the Ghibdul lair.

These magic beings could fly for short distances at low altitudes of less than three meters from the ground, and now they swept through the forest searching for their prey. When they found them, they tied them up roughly with strong vines and sneered at their victims. How could such pathetic creatures ever have seemed like a threat?

Two Ghibdul warriors grabbed the travelers as if they were nothing more than packages, and the creatures flew merrily back to their city.

The room seemed to spin around him. Where was he? What was happening? The young hovalyn had no idea. He tried to remember recent events, but his mind was still in a fog. He forced himself to keep his eyes open. He did not remember losing consciousness. Then he realized that his wrists and legs were bound, and that he was tied to a sort of chair covered with a greenish moss like lichen. Still drowsy, he did not even try to free himself. He was in a strange room with dirty white walls, along with Elfohrys, who was unconscious and also tied with the same dark vines.

Slowly the young man's mind cleared completely. This experience was like the one two years before, when he had woken up in a field in the middle of nowhere, except that this time, thank goodness, he could still remember everything that had happened before he'd fallen asleep in the clearing. He studied the room more attentively. The light was dim. Besides the two bizarre chairs, the place had no other furniture and told him nothing about his captors. He tried to wriggle free, to break his bonds, but in vain. On the contrary, the vines gripped him all the more tightly.

Then Elfohrys woke up, just as confused as his companion.

"Where are we?" he asked groggily.

"I don't know. You can't remember how we got here either?"

"I can't recall a thing."

The young man heaved a sigh of relief. So he wasn't alone in having no recollection of their capture, and there must be some explanation for their loss of memory.

The door opened with a sudden crash. Treading heavily, a Ghibdul haughtily entered the room. He was short and stooped, but this did not make his appearance any more reassuring. A kind of natural armor like a dark green shield covered his body. The only parts not concealed were his repulsive hands, sharp-clawed feet, and his purplish neck and head. His wrinkled face was particularly frightening: his nose had three nostrils, and his eyes, two folded slits, were an unclean, muddy color, glittering with intelligence and cruelty. His mouth, of the same green as his armor, was twisted and so translucent it was almost invisible. Unruly hair, like the vines binding the two prisoners, stuck out from under the Ghibdul's rusty helmet, and from his back grew two flimsy, blackish wings, now folded.

He was terrifying.

"A Ghibdul," Elfohrys observed aloud.

"Do you have a problem with that, prisoner?" growled the creature.

"Where are we?" asked the Nameless One. "What do you want from us?"

"Be quiet, vermin. It is beneath my dignity to speak to beasts such as you. No one, no prey, has ever had that honor."

"I would willingly have done without it," grumbled Elfohrys.

"Shut up! I speak; you listen. If you do not obey me, I will behead you here and now, and you will have to wait until Death's strike is over for me to kill you for good!"

The prospect of waiting with their heads cut off to be dispatched at some uncertain date by this gruesome creature persuaded the two captives to remain silent.

"Right," continued the Ghibdul in his hollow voice. "This is the situation. You are our prisoners, and you have no chance of escaping. First, you should know that you are within our city, which I am sure must seem breathtaking to you inferior animals, unaccustomed as you are to our refined civilization. In a few hours, you will be fed. Then we will bring you to a place that will delight your uneducated minds—"

"What place?" asked Elfohrys without thinking.

"Silence!" thundered the Ghibdul. "How dare you defy me, inferior being!"

"I didn't mean to," replied Elfohrys placidly.

"You miserable creature! If you only knew how much I long to tear you limb from limb this very moment. . . ."

The Ghibdul went over to Elfohrys and passed his hand lightly across the Clohryun's cheek, slicing it open with curving claws. Golden blood welled up on the prisoner's silvery skin, but he never made a sound.

It was the Nameless One who spoke to the Ghibdul.

"You'll be sorry for that, I promise you."

"You dare threaten me?"

Surprisingly, their tormentor seemed almost thoughtful, even curious.

"It isn't an empty threat," continued the young knight. "I always prefer to give fair warning."

"I'll show you on the spot what I'm capable of," declared the Ghibdul.

"That's fine with me," said the hovalyn firmly.

"We'll fight barehanded, but I will spare your life, so as not to disobey my orders."

"Very well," replied his adversary, not in the least intimidated.

The Ghibdul uttered a few unintelligible syllables, and the vines binding the young man untied themselves. Elfohrys glanced uneasily at his friend.

The Nameless One knew that one or two swipes from those fearsome claws would be enough to defeat him, yet he stepped forward serenely, almost nonchalantly.

The Ghibdul's expression changed hideously, stretching his face with what could only be interpreted as an evil smile. Without warning, he lunged at the young man, who seemed so frail and harmless in comparison, and his hands slashed repeatedly through the air, but whenever his opponent seemed within reach, the agile young knight would evade his attacker. The Ghibdul gradually ran out of breath, but not wanting to admit defeat, he kept trying to wound the hovalyn.

Elfohrys watched his nimble young friend with admiration as he skillfully dodged every blow.

At last, the panting Ghibdul muttered a few incomprehensible words that propelled the hovalyn back into his chair, where the vines twined around him once again.

"Man," said the Ghibdul in a harsh voice with a hint of grudging respect, "if you have managed to avoid my attacks barehanded, that does not make you in any way superior to me."

"I never claimed I was," replied his prisoner evenly, "but you have no reason to think me inferior to you, either."

"Wait and see what we Ghibduls can do! Our telepathic strength is unequaled and, armed, we are formidable!"

"Very interesting," observed the young knight.

Visibly offended, the magical creature left without another word.

"Why did you challenge the Ghibdul?" asked Elfohrys reproachfully.

"I wasn't going to let him attack you without saying anything."

"A rash reaction to a few drops of my blood! I have strong natural defenses, and my wounds will swiftly heal without leaving any marks. But you, you've just earned the enmity of that Ghibdul, which won't vanish so quickly, believe me!"

"Well, he didn't seem particularly well disposed toward us from the beginning," replied the hovalyn lightly.

Frustrated by the bonds imprisoning them, the two captives tried in vain to free themselves as the minutes ticked by, and they could not help wondering anxiously what fate lay in store for them.

When the door finally opened, it was a woman who entered. Elfohrys and the Nameless One stared at her in amazement. She was human! Clothed in a clumsy patchwork of fabrics made from forest plants, the woman was dirty, and her bare feet, like her hands, were covered with scars. Her face, although disagreeable, nevertheless showed clearly that she was human. She had high, prominent cheekbones, an aggressive gleam in her slanting black eyes, and thin lips. Her complexion was dull and her flat nose seemed to take up most of her morose face. Tangled brown hair stuck together with mud and filth fell to her broad shoulders.

Setting down a wooden tray bearing a few fruits, she undid the vines binding the two prisoners' hands, complaining all the while.

"Eat," she said in a gravelly voice, "but don't be thinkin' 'bout escapin'! You can do as you like, but those ties round your feet, they won't come undone!"

"You're human?" asked the young knight politely.

"Yeah, but the Ghibduls need servants like me. Women lost in the forest—they take them into service. They ain't mean to me, not 't all."

"What's your name?" asked the hovalyn, trying to strike up a conversation with the woman and gain her confidence.

"Naïlde. Eat, don't ask questions! I ain't to speak to you. I 'ave it good 'ere, and I don't 'elp prisoners. You think I'd run 'way, maybe? Well, sorry—nah."

"You let people of your kind die? You don't feel bad hearing them scream under torture?" asked Elfohrys.

"The Ghibduls treat me better 'n humans did, so me, I serve 'em right, that's all."

With that, Naïlde swore and spat contemptuously at the young hovalyn's feet. Then, with a strand of spittle still on her lips and a sour, disdainful look on her face, she turned on her heel and left, slamming the door behind her.

"Unbelievable," marveled Elfohrys. "That woman has even adopted the Ghibduls' charming customs!"

"Who knows what her life among her own kind was like," replied the Nameless One kindly. "Before becoming an inhuman woman, she must have been a simple soul, perhaps misunderstood. She has probably suffered a great deal. We cannot say what comfort she has found among the Ghibduls, but judging from what she says, she's satisfied with her life here."

Elfohrys looked at his friend curiously. He was speaking sympathetically about a woman who had just refused to set him free! The nature of humans, concluded the Clohryun, is definitely even more incomprehensible than I've been told.

The young man was quietly eating some of the fruit brought by Naïlde. When he'd had enough, he handed the tray to Elfohrys, who devoured everything that was left. Since his hands were still free, the hovalyn tried to remove the bonds around his legs, but with no success.

"Ah, you humans," sighed Elfohrys, almost resignedly. "Ever hopeful! If you ask me, it's what ensures your survival. No matter how many times you're told it's no use, you keep trying anyway."

When Naïlde returned to collect the tray, the Nameless One held his breath, wondering if the servant might have changed her mind, won over by pity. Elfohrys noticed the gleam of hope in his eye and thought, Still just as naive, still trusting in others. Humans are convinced that they're filled with goodness even when they're striving to do one another in. Strange. . . .

Naïlde let loose another barrage of insults at the young man, whom she seemed to take a personal satisfaction in humiliating. Clearly she had not changed her mind one whit, and the disappointed hovalyn realized he'd failed to convince her to set him free.

Grumbling, the servant left the room.

The two prisoners began to feel apprehensive again after Naïlde had gone, and almost immediately, four imposing Ghibduls appeared, one of whom muttered a few words that released the captives from their bonds.

"Follow us," ordered a Ghibdul gruffly.

As they were led through somber rooms toward an exit, the two companions were able to observe the building where they had been imprisoned: its bizarre architecture lent it a dark air of isolation, and yet, inside, the gloomy place was swarming with Ghibduls.

The captives were escorted by their jailers through narrow, winding streets. They soon discovered what no outsider could have suspected: the active and organized Ghibdul capital, hidden away. Its location had clearly been carefully chosen, for this small city was surrounded by huge trees that formed a natural defense.

An immense building gradually appeared before them, and the Ghibduls escorting them smiled proudly when they caught sight of it. It was built of stones painted black, decorated with embellishments, and resembled a theater.

The small party entered a crowded hall where striking sculptures and paintings revealed the Ghibduls to be capable of fine and original art—a talent that would have astonished any outsider.

The jailers escorted their prisoners through the throng and up endless stairs until they reached a copper door. Opening it, they thrust in their charges, slammed the door shut, and left.

Without even the vaguest notion of what was happening to them, the two companions tumbled into a void. After falling through a sort of spongy bubble, they landed unhurt—to a wave of applause.

Dumbfounded, they rubbed their eyes at an incredible sight: the interior of a gigantic theater, very elegant and well lit, where thousands of Ghibduls were comfortably ensconced in seats covered with dark velvet. Newcomers were streaming into the audience from all directions. The theater was elliptical in shape with countless rows of spectators leading up to a ceiling that depicted the forest beneath an azure sky. In the center of the theater was a spacious stage atop a short, wide marble column surrounded by transparent glass, enabling the spectators to see the stage from any direction.

The only problem was that Elfohrys and the Nameless

One found themselves on this very stage. Looking up at the ceiling, they could see the almost invisible trapdoor through which they had plummeted into the heart of this theater.

"Elfohrys, where are we?"

"I have no idea, and it wouldn't help a bit if I did."

"But this is incredible!" said the hovalyn. "Everyone says the Ghibduls are barbarians, and here we are in the middle of an unimaginable place!"

"You know, Nameless One, it's a shame, but I don't think we're ever going to get a chance to tell anyone about it."

Ghibduls were flying around the theater offering refreshments to the audience. The concept of money was alien to them: buying, selling—none of that existed. Nature provided them with everything.

The young hovalyn noticed that a small section of the theater was a standing-room area reserved for a few dozen coarse women, some of them human, and even at a distance he recognized Naïlde among them, screaming and shaking her fist, perhaps at him.

The lights went out. A powerful voice echoed through the theater.

"Welcome, my dear Ghibdul friends! Today I have the honor of presenting to you an authentic Clohryun and a man—a hovalyn, would you believe! Who will be the victor? How long will they hold out? The betting is open. As usual they will undergo the trials we have prepared for your entertainment. And so I wish you a pleasant afternoon—and I hope you enjoy the show!"

The audience clapped enthusiastically.

Elfohrys and the Nameless One exchanged worried looks. Before they could say a word, while the spectators were still applauding their entrance, they both felt a sharp pain stab them in the left arm. The young hovalyn already had a wound inflicted in battle by the Bumblinks, and now this wound reopened and began to bleed. He stifled a cry, but almost at the same time came another attack, this time battering his whole body. It caused no wound, but he could hardly keep himself from collapsing and writhing in agony on the stage.

The Ghibduls laughed, commenting on the scene with amusement.

The expression on Elfohrys's face showed that he also was in atrocious pain, and at the third assault, directed at the left leg of the two victims, the Clohryun fell fainting to the ground.

The audience booed him disdainfully.

The young hovalyn was staggering, seriously wounded in

the leg. The unbearable odor of his own blood was choking him, strangling him; he was drowning in it, and his eyes rolled upward with anger. Why were these Ghibduls so savagely eager to see him suffer? Determined to behave with dignity, he stayed on his feet while his left arm was lacerated by an unseen power. Murmurs of astonishment began to ripple through the crowd.

A fresh barrage of bodily pain was launched at the hovalyn, knocking him down, to shouts of disappointment from the audience.

The Nameless One immediately plucked up his courage and strength, however, and staggered to his feet once more. His eyes shone with such determination that the spectators were shaken.

When he felt an invisible dagger pierce his abdomen, the hovalyn did not flinch. After all, he wasn't risking anything, because Death was on strike. All he had to do was resist the attacks. But he was exhausted, and when agony surged through his body again, he had to lean against the glass wall surrounding the stage. With a last effort he tried to draw himself up, to shout a threat, something brave and dignified that would restore a little of his pride but everything was growing hazy around him: images, sounds, smells—all of his perceptions were fading, vanishing, leaving only suffering.

Still he resisted, when all of a sudden the same voice from before resounded throughout the theater: "The moment has come—it is time to choose."

A thrill of excitement swept through the crowd. The Nameless One made a superhuman effort to stay on his feet. Everything seemed so distant. . . .

"Hovalyn!" continued the voice. "Kneel, renounce what you are, give up the fight. You can never vanquish us. If you submit, your torture will cease, you will be one of us. We know the identity you seek so desperately. We will reveal it to you. You will have a place among us. But if you defy us and refuse this offer, the pain will torment you to the point of madness. And when Death ends her strike, we will kill you. So, do you admit defeat? Will you serve us?"

"Never," gasped the Nameless One.

A new wave of pain flooded instantly through him.

A distant voice, solemn and harsh, but filled with admiration, then echoed through the theater.

"It's him. . . . It's him! Stop, it's him!"

The Nameless One fell unconscious.

18

THE NALYSS

THE SUN HAD BARELY RISEN WHEN THE THREE travelers woke up. They ate a meager breakfast; Amber tried tasting a strange fruit that turned out to be delicious. No one spoke, for they were still quite tired.

Opal was the first to see the two girls coming toward them. Their fresh, dainty faces seemed quite carefree, yet Amber could not help noticing their conceited, almost disdainful expressions. It was impossible to tell how old they were. They both had short brown hair, attractively tousled, but one had liquid brown eyes while the other's eyes were periwinkle blue—with a gleam of malice. They looked very much alike: small, narrow, slightly upturned noses; full lips set in an innocent pout. Their features and attitude suggested that the girls were charming and angelic, but they could not disguise a certain arrogance.

At first the two newcomers simply studied the three travelers in silence. Then the blue-eyed girl piped up, "Loorine! Do you think they're humans? Real live humans?"

"Could be," replied the other in a rather snooty tone. "What luck!"

"I'm definitely alive," announced Jade dryly. "You might take that into account while talking about us."

"You're right, Mairénith," said Loorine. "They are humans!"

"Thanks for noticing," snarled Jade.

Amber and Opal examined the strange girls attentively, feeling more irritated than intrigued by the contempt in their voices.

"How happy I am!" cried Mairénith, batting her long, curving black eyelashes.

"We're so pleased to meet you," declared Loorine, with a smile that revealed her perfect white teeth.

"I think you're pretty!" said Mairénith merrily. "Don't you agree, Loorine?"

"Yes, very pretty."

"Thank you," said Jade, "but would you please stop making fun of us?"

"Very pretty," repeated Loorine. "We've never seen the like before, have we?"

"No," said Mairénith. "Jade, tell me, do you find me pretty?"

"How do you know my name?"

"I just do. I'm a Nalyss, and nothing less. So, do you think we're pretty?" she continued in a wheedling voice.

By now Jade, Amber, and Opal were wondering just who these visitors could possibly be.

"Why do you ask?" said Amber.

"I really want to know," replied Mairénith fretfully.

"Yes, you're pretty," said Jade in exasperation. "But you're very weird, and if I were you, I wouldn't be so conceited."

Amber and Opal smiled fleetingly to hear Jade mention her own greatest flaw.

"She thinks we're pretty!" crowed Mairénith in delight, as if she hadn't heard anything but that.

"Of course we are!" agreed Loorine.

A third girl then appeared. She was as lovely as the other two but did not resemble them, and it was easier to guess her age, which couldn't have been more than fifteen. She seemed delicate but not frail, with exquisite features, a glowing complexion, bright red lips, and silky hair that hung down to her slim waist. Her gaze seemed so pure and innocent that it was positively unsettling.

"Oh, Loorine!" groaned Mairénith.

"Such ugliness!" wailed her companion.

"I can't bear it," moaned Mairénith, on the verge of tears.

"Go away, quickly, you horrid creature!" shouted

Loorine. "Leave us alone! Don't come near these travelers!"

Then, as if appalled by some repulsive vision, Mairénith and Loorine took to their heels.

"They are really something else," said Amber, who would have burst out laughing if she hadn't been so astonished.

"You said it!" agreed Jade.

"Anyway, why did they run off like that?" wondered Amber. "I thought they'd seen some dreadful monster— what a racket they were making! Honestly, I just can't figure it out at all."

Jade merely shrugged, while the newcomer approached and said with a smile, "My name is Janëlle."

"Delighted to hear it," observed Jade sourly.

"The girls you just saw are Nalyss. They're rather bizarre, aren't they?"

Janëlle sat next to the three travelers and began to tell them about the Nalyss, who are not uncommon in Fairytale. They are always female and never live beyond the age of thirty. Extremely narcissistic, they spend their entire lives in passionate adoration of their beauty, an obsession so all-consuming that they have to avoid seeing themselves in a mirror or on the surface of a lake, for fear that they will never be able to tear themselves away from their reflections.

Janëlle neglected to mention that not many people

could actually see them. The Nalyss have an unusual gift that even they do not fully appreciate: they can see a person's inner beauty, and see it even more clearly than simple physical attractiveness. Only people who are beautiful both on the inside and the outside can see the Nalyss, and anyone else is repulsive to them.

The Nalyss spend their lives trying to meet as many people as possible who will confirm their own beauty. They are superficial and unintelligent and they amuse themselves by captivating men they find worthy of their attention in order to drive them insane with love—and, occasionally, to have children by them, who are always born Nalyss.

At the end of their existence, very few of them realize that they have vainly pursued a meaningless ideal, that their beauty has brought them nothing, and that they have quite simply forgotten to live.

Her story told, Janëlle let a long silence fall.

"And you, who are you?" asked Jade, breaking the spell.

"I am Janëlle, and I guide people to their destination in return for food and a little pleasant company."

"In that case, beat it," said Jade, who had no idea why she was reacting so nastily.

"No, don't go!" cried Amber indignantly. "Janëlle, could

you take us to Oonagh? We don't know anything at all about Fairytale, and we're a little lost."

"Of course I'll take you," replied Janëlle, beaming with pleasure.

Saying nothing, Opal simply studied the smiling girl; she wasn't happy about her arrival, but she felt no hostility toward her, either.

The party set out again, with Amber and Opal on one horse, Jade and Janëlle on the other.

It soon became clear that Janëlle was casting a pall on the three travelers' spirits. Not daring to trust her, they kept quiet to avoid giving away anything important. And yet, Janëlle truly did seem inoffensive, so Amber decided to talk to her.

Janëlle quickly showed herself to be a nice, normal girl, and she explained to Amber that, like her three new companions, she was fourteen years old. She was very poor, and instead of moping in her village, she had preferred to explore Fairytale by becoming a guide.

"At your age?" marveled Amber. "I didn't know that such dire poverty could exist here!"

"Unfortunately, yes. Wherever there is life, there cannot always be happiness."

Despite the furious looks Jade gave her, Amber

responded to Janëlle's friendly overtures by telling her own story, from the beginning. She had just reached the part when she had first seen her Stone when Jade interrupted her angrily.

"Be quiet, Amber! You're not supposed to talk about that!"

Amber's sweet face clouded over instantly.

"Jade, it's not for you to tell me what I must or must not do. I can decide for myself. If you can't manage to trust anyone, that's sad, but it's your problem. Not mine. I respect your opinions, so don't judge mine. You should mind your own business, Miss Princess, and let other people take care of themselves."

Although Amber didn't flinch at Jade's wounded expression, she was secretly stunned by her own words.

"It's funny when you realize how wrong you can be," said Jade in a cold, numb voice. "You take the risk of respecting someone, even though she might be an enemy, a real danger to you, but instead of heeding such warnings, you think you're creating a fragile friendship, a mutual understanding. And then you're forced to admit what you'd thought you could ignore: suddenly you discover an enemy where you would have sworn you had a friend."

Startled by the unusually heated argument between

her companions, Opal tried clumsily to bring the conversation back to safer ground.

"What happened while I was still unconscious? How come I didn't die? And is Adrien all right? Where is he? I dreamed . . . that he was in a uniform, and I had the feeling that he was going to leave."

"That's true," said Amber. "I'd forgotten that you don't know the latest developments."

And although her voice still showed her irritation, Amber began to tell Opal about everything that she had missed.

Jade rode along without looking up; although she didn't want to admit it, she didn't feel like her usual self. She was gradually growing used to Janëlle and was beginning, not to accept her presence, but simply to forget she was there.

The girls rode through several villages without incident. After Amber finished relating to Opal all that had happened during her coma, there was an awkward silence, which Janëlle tried unsuccessfully to dispel.

After a few hours, Amber's exhausted horse sent her a weak telepathic message, asking her if he might rest.

"We have to stop," she announced, and although they all agreed to halt there in the middle of a rugged plain, they could still feel a certain tension in the atmosphere.

"Do you think you're special because you can read a horse's thoughts?" asked Jade snidely.

"At least I don't think I'm the center of the universe," Amber shot back.

"Stop it, you two!" exclaimed Opal, growing more and more baffled. "Something weird is going on. Maybe we should use our Stones."

"That's right, you aren't strong enough to take responsibility for yourself," replied Amber. "You always have to ask for help."

"So you think you can hurt me?" Opal asked Amber. "Too bad, you're wrong. I hope you aren't going to start crying—because I know what a sensitive girl you are, so touchy-feely with everyone, and it would be so sad to see you all teary. Oh, sorry—how can I be saying such things to you, when you're just so perfect? Of course, I wouldn't dare mention that you're just a poor, ignorant, and sentimental peasant!"

Opal couldn't believe she'd just spewed out those words—they had poured forth of their own accord, harsh and uncontrollable. But now she wasn't sorry that she'd said them, because blind hatred was starting to grow inside her.

The girls set out once more. Speaking soothingly, Janëlle

tried to start a peaceful conversation, but it was hopeless: the other three lashed out at one another with increasing venom. Things deteriorated when Amber and Jade reined in their horses after two hours, saying it was time to rest again. They had hardly dismounted when they flew into a fury, slapping each other in the face. Opal joined in the brawl as well, giving a few vigorous thumps of her own.

At first Janëlle called out to them, but to no effect. Then she yelled her head off. It was a waste of time. She waded into the fray, receiving a flurry of vicious blows. Her slender body seemed to falter for a moment; then, with unexpected strength and determination, she separated the three girls.

With her jet-black hair in wild disorder, her clothes torn, Jade seemed beside herself, red-faced and menacing. A few drops of blood beaded a shallow cut on her cheek. Opal had come out of it with only a few scratches, and the look in her eyes was more inscrutable than ever. The pain of her wound had flared up again, and she kept her head down to hide her feelings. As for Amber, she was fighting back tears. Her bruised lower lip was split, and she tasted the hot, disagreeable bitterness of blood in her mouth.

They glared at one another.

The situation had become unbearable.

*　　*　　*

Somehow the girls managed to mount their horses and continue their journey, but the air was filled with palpable tension and bitterness as they struggled to hold their angry tongues.

When night fell, bringing an end to a difficult and tiring day, the four girls stopped at the edge of a meadow, for Janëlle had persuaded the others to spend the night outdoors rather than in an unfamiliar village.

Unable to bear even sharing some food, Jade and Opal stalked off across the field in different directions to spend the night on their own.

Amber was alone with Janëlle. She felt no resentment toward their young guide, whose presence didn't affect her bad mood one way or the other. Janëlle began to tell Amber about her past, how she had come to be alone, working as a guide. Janëlle's story was so similar to her own that Amber found herself opening up to the other girl and pouring out her grief over her mother's death. She was relieved to have found a real friend, after being so let down by Jade and Opal.

When they grew tired, the two friends decided to go to sleep, promising to continue their conversation the next day. Amber slept heavily, without any dreams.

The sky was sprinkled with stars; the moon shone faintly. In the middle of the night, the silence was broken by a stifled cry. Amber awoke suddenly, gasping for breath; she felt a burning sensation spread throughout her body, and slowly, painfully, she struggled to her feet.

"What's happening?" she moaned. "I feel so terrible!"

Janëlle did not reply. Her expression had changed into one of loathing and malevolence. She bent down and tried to pick up something in the thick grass, then straightened up with a shriek. It was impossible to deny: her eyes were flashing with rage.

"Janëlle!" gasped Amber, mesmerized.

"Leave me alone!" cried the other girl in a shrill, hysterical voice.

"What's the matter with you?"

"Can't you tell? Don't you want to understand?"

Janëlle slowly held out her clenched fist, then opened her fingers to reveal a palm disfigured by burns. At that moment, Amber saw her as the Nalyss had perceived her—as everyone would have seen her if her appearance had been the reflection of her soul: oily skin, messy black hair, dark eyes buried in puffy cheeks, a piggy nose, a massive and ungainly figure. Her eyes glittered with wickedness, and all her features betrayed a desire to destroy: she had become the incarnation of hatred.

"It's your fault!" she screamed, as if demented.

"But—what is?"

"Everything! You don't dare see what's right in front of you? I hate you. . . . I hate you!"

Amber felt sick. Her eyes filled with tears. She didn't understand anything anymore, and didn't want to.

"You have everything for yourself, you're the one I should have been!" wailed Janëlle. "You've stolen my place! You've stolen my life!"

"That's insane," stammered Amber.

"Of course, it's easy for you to say that. Me, I'm just a poor miserable girl, I have no right to be important—that's what you think."

"No, no, not at all!"

"You still don't get it? Then I'll help you. Let's go back to the beginning. I meet three girls, so I stop, and from what I hear them say, I realize that they've seen some Nalyss who ran away when they saw me coming! Of course, these three are perfect enough to have seen them, but not me!"

"I—I didn't know," whispered Amber, who felt the burning sensation in her body grow worse as her world crumbled around her.

"So," continued Janëlle, "I decide to make friends with them. I want to show them that I, too, have a right to exist, to be appreciated."

"I never said you didn't—"

"But these three girls ignore me."

"That's not true!"

"They have everything on their side. Life has given them so much, and me, nothing. I feel violent anger growing inside me: it fills me, possesses me, until it takes me over completely. I have to get rid of it. I concentrate, and with an ease I've never known before, I expel my hatred. It over-flows . . . into the soul of another."

"Jade!" said Amber.

"But this hatred keeps rising in me, so to control myself I shift it to you, then to the other girl, Opal, isn't that her name? The anger gradually enslaves me and each of you in turn."

"Why? We didn't do anything to you!" protested Amber, choking with misery.

"Then you confide in me. I invent the story of my so-called life and you believe me, feel sorry for me. I hate your goody-goody feelings, your sympathetic manner. I was dying to spit out the truth, to tell you how I've infected people with hatred and brought about deaths, caused wars.

When you told me about your Stone, I realized who you were. And then I thought I was going to explode with rage. I wanted to outdo you, humiliate you, annihilate you."

"No!" cried Amber miserably, still refusing to accept the truth.

"Tonight I tried to steal your Stone, but I couldn't: it burned my hand. And you! You woke up, so trusting, with that perfect, smart, unbearable look on your face."

Amber couldn't say a word.

"What do you think? That I'm some tormented soul? That I turn to evil simply to escape from my problems? No. Evil nourishes me, gives me power! Without evil, I'm nothing. I serve it, but it consoles me, transforms me, makes me invulnerable! I need evil. When I see others suffer, when I feel evil possess me, I grow strong! With no more need to hide behind simpering smiles, to force myself to be someone else, to seem nice. Evil lets me be myself."

"Why are you telling me all this?"

"Because I know that it hurts you. My words wound you, make your bruised soul bleed—and I love that. You thought you were better than I am? You aren't! You thought I was your friend? I was just the opposite, one of your most fervent enemies! Your tears give me incredible joy. You think I've betrayed you? Well, I have no regret: I do as I please, I follow my own nature. I don't flinch at the slippery world I'm forced to live in; I create evil, and I live off it."

With these words, Janëlle smiled triumphantly and left satisfied.

Amber thought she vaguely glimpsed a horseman in the distance, watching the scene, but that image could only have been an illusion, a mirage in the night.

She looked in the grass for her Stone, which had turned warm and comforting again. The bitterness and burning in her heart had vanished with Janëlle, yet her cheeks were still wet with tears, like pearls of deep dismay.

Paris: Present Day

I was growing frailer, weaker. I barely touched the food the nurses brought me. For months I'd refused to look in a mirror; I could just imagine seeing myself: thin, shaking, my bones sticking out, my face drawn. I didn't dare confront the despair in my eyes. I wanted to keep the image of Joa, not the specter of an invalid huddled in fear. When I closed my eyes tightly enough, I still saw myself the way I used to be. The image would come to me slowly, and it was growing more and more blurry as the days went by. Then I was somebody else: Joa. . . .

It hurt to remember how things used to be, and tears would sting my eyes. I had tried to forget everything, to file my past away in the depths of memory, and I had thought I'd succeeded. I wanted to accept my fate.

But the dream dredged up the past—the three girls reminded me of how I had once been—and at the same time began sketching out the future. I thought I was strong enough, tough enough to resist the dream. I was wrong. Although I wouldn't admit it to myself,

I felt stirrings of renewed hope. And yet, this whole story was only a dream—this tale that was bringing me back to life was something my tormented mind had invented from nothing. I was almost afraid to think about it, as if my memories, my thoughts, my feelings might change the sparkling colors of the dream, muddling them until they grew pale, faint, and faded away. The dream seemed so important to me that I dreaded feeling it slip away from my memory. I wanted it to continue, forever. Although I wouldn't let myself admit this, unconsciously I believed the dream was true, I felt it was true, I wanted it to be true.

But my illness continued to destroy me. I was in pain, and the dream, which carried me far from my reality, renewed my pain whenever I left it and returned to my hospital bed. The more I wished to live, the more I suffered in my struggle against death. Once again I began to reject that fate and to believe in the illusion of hope; naive, perhaps, but I was happier that way.

19

The Chosen One

THE NAMELESS ONE OPENED HIS EYES AND quickly regained consciousness. His injuries had disappeared. He no longer felt any pain or saw any trace of the deep wounds he had sustained. He realized that he was in the same room as before, a narrow room with bare walls. And though he was still sitting on the strange chair of green moss, his limbs were no longer restrained by bonds. Next to him, Elfohrys seemed unhurt as well, although he was still tied up.

"Ah! Nameless One!" Elfohrys cried. "Finally, you've come round!"

"But—the theater, the agony . . ."

"Excuse me? You must still be in shock."

"I didn't dream it," murmured the puzzled hovalyn.

"A few hours ago, after Naïlde left, some Ghibduls came."

"I know."

"They surrounded you and started chanting a strange

spell. You fainted, became agitated, and babbled some incomprehensible sounds. Then they stood around you without a word for about half an hour. I was beginning to get really worried! You were still unconscious when they left. I shouted, I tried to help you. At last, after two hours, the vines imprisoning you untied themselves, and you seemed to become more peaceful."

Perplexed, the haggard young man stared at his intact limbs, unmarked, save for the old wound on his right arm. He took his head in his hands. Was his memory beginning to play tricks on him? After eradicating his past, was it betraying him anew, conjuring up an imaginary present?

Before he could think any further, three Ghibduls entered the room. Their monstrous faces were twisted into affable expressions, while their lips tried vainly to form smiles. Approaching the knight, one of the visitors silently held out to him a long object wrapped in an immaculate white cloth. The young man reached for it with a tentative hand.

"Take it," said a Ghibdul encouragingly, in a harsh voice tinged with humility, respect, and admiration.

Unwrapping the object, the Nameless One was astonished—it was his enchanted sword!

"If you will accept them," continued the Ghibdul, "we

would like to offer you our apologies, honorable hovalyn."

Elfohrys hooted with laughter, which drew scowls from the Ghibduls.

"Perhaps you could let us go now," suggested Elfohrys gaily. "We're quite touched by your sudden change of heart, but—"

"Quiet, wretch!" ordered the Ghibdul who had returned the sword and who clearly had the most authority.

"I forbid you to treat Elfohrys like that!" protested the hovalyn indignantly.

"If such is your wish," mumbled the disconcerted Ghibdul.

"I think that you might offer us some explanation," continued the young man, still bewildered but determined to take advantage of this unexpected development.

"We entered your mind and staged a simulated experience, using images that were already in your thoughts but of whose existence you were unaware. And we added a few elements of our own."

"So everything I thought I saw and felt was false?"

"From the moment you thought you had left this room," confirmed the Ghibdul. "It was a necessary and effective test. We are particularly gifted at this sort of painless manipulation."

"Painless," sighed their victim. "That word may not mean the same thing to everyone, but personally, I did not consider the invasion of my mind to be either pleasant or harmless!"

The Ghibdul was so close to him that the young man could smell the creature's fetid breath, and he turned his head aside when his visitor spoke again.

"There were some doubts about you. What we had at first suspected seemed unlikely, but we were determined to settle the question. And in entering your mind, we were able to confirm our initial suspicions, our hopes. . . ."

"Oh, so you are actually capable of hoping?" said Elfohrys sarcastically. "Well, we learn something every day."

"Hovalyn, you are the one we have long awaited. What is your name?"

"I don't have one," confessed the knight. "I am the Nameless One."

The Ghibduls did not seem troubled by this news.

"You are the only one to have ever completely withstood the, uh, the mental torture we inflicted on you. We are truly sorry to have put you through that."

"Well, you certainly weren't very subtle about it."

"But it was necessary," said the Ghibdul earnestly. "Even among ourselves, no one has ever lasted that long under

I can hardly hear my heartbeat anymore. Death is waiting for me. Impatiently.

"Listen to me, she's very weak," the nurse is saying. "She hasn't got long now."

"You can't keep me from seeing her!" the young man protests anxiously. "I have to be with her. She has to live!" There was a burning determination in his eyes, perhaps even mixed with a faint flicker of hope.

"I'm afraid it might be too late," explains the nurse.

She looks at the young man. He has tousled brown hair, desperate eyes.

"Didn't you ever come to see her before?" she asks.

"Once," he says bitterly. "Let me see her," he pleads.

The nurse thinks about it for a moment.

"Go on in," she says gently, "but don't be long."

I don't know if Eli will come. But I look at the sun in the palm of my hand and I believe. I believe in the impossible, I believe in my dream, in my vision of the future. I believe in Elyador. I'm still hoping. Simply hoping.

Death is nearby. Too bad. She'll wait.

I'll live. Because I have to. Because I want to. I've been dreaming. Now, I'd rather live, even if it comes to the same thing.

My dream gave life back to me. Now I must give dreams back to life.